MARRIED LIFE

Sergio Pitol

Translated from the Spanish by G. B. Henson

DEEP VELLUM PUBLISHING
DALLAS, TEXAS

Deep Vellum Publishing
3000 Commerce Street, Dallas, Texas 75226
deepvellum.org · @deepvellum

Deep Vellum is a 501c3 nonprofit literary arts organization founded in 2013 with the mission to bring the world into conversation through literature.

Originally published in Spanish as *La vida conjugal*
Editorial Anagrama, Mexico City, Mexico, 1991.

First English edition, 2025

Support for this publication has been provided in part by grants from the Texas Commission on the Arts, the City of Dallas Office of Arts and Culture, and the Addy Foundation.

Paperback ISBN: 978-1-64605-407-7 | Ebook ISBN: 978-1-64605-408-4

LIBRARY OF CONGRESS CATALOGING-IN-PUBLICATION DATA

Names: Pitol, Sergio, 1933-2018 author | Henson, George translator
Title: Married life / Sergio Pitol ; translated from the Spanish by George Henson.
Other titles: Vida conyugal. English
Description: First English edition. | Dallas, Texas : Deep Vellum Publishing, 2025.
Identifiers: LCCN 2025029594 (print) | LCCN 2025029595 (ebook) | ISBN 9781646054077 trade paperback | ISBN 9781646054084 ebook
Subjects: LCSH: Marriage--Fiction | LCGFT: Fiction | Novels
Classification: LCC PQ7298.26.I8 V513 2025 (print) | LCC PQ7298.26.I8 (ebook)
LC record available at https://lccn.loc.gov/2025029594
LC ebook record available at https://lccn.loc.gov/2025029595

Exterior design by Kit Schluter
Interior layout and typesetting by KGT

PRINTED IN THE UNITED STATES OF AMERICA

PRAISE FOR SERGIO PITOL

"Pitol is not just our best living storyteller, he is also the strongest renovator of our literature."
—Álvaro Enrigue, author of *Sudden Death*

"One of Mexico's most culturally complex and composite writers."
—Publishers Weekly

"Certainly the strangest, most unfathomable and eccentric . . . His voice reverberates beyond the margins of his books."
—Valeria Luiselli, author of *Faces in the Crowd*

"Reading him, one has the impression . . . of being before the greatest Spanish-language writer of our time." **—Enrique Vila-Matas**

"His literature reflects the droll and ironic constant of his observations . . . Pitol knew how to see others, and he managed to reconcile and reflect very different worlds."
—Elena Poniatowska, author of *The Heart of the Artichoke*

"Pitol is a writer of another kind: his importance lies on the page, in the creation of his own world, in his ability to shed light on the world."
—Daniel Saldaña Paris, author of *Among Strange Victims*

"Pitol's short stories, essays and crime novels merge fiction with memoir in an imaginative swirl of contemplation and reflection."
—Paulina Villegas, *The New York Times*

"Reading Sergio Pitol will make any serious writer want to write—and write better . . . In Pitol's life and his writing, neither images nor thoughts flow naturally and automatically to their logical associations." ***—3:AM Magazine***

OTHER BOOKS BY SERGIO PITOL
AVAILABLE IN ENGLISH TRANSLATION

The Art of Flight

The Journey

The Magician of Vienna

Mephisto's Waltz

The Love Parade

Taming the Divine Heron

CONTENTS

Sergio Pitol, Universal Writer

Mark Haber

I first discovered Sergio Pitol in 2015 when I read *The Art of Flight* in George Henson's peerless translation. I was a bookseller, obsessed with literature in translation, especially Latin American literature and, more specifically, Mexican literature. Reading *The Art of Flight* felt akin to landing on the shores of an immense and unexplored continent: lush, strange, both daunting and inspiring. It was elegant, worldly, humorous, profound; it mixed autobiography with travel writing and philosophy, even a dash of fiction. The language was worldly, learned, but also approachable, generous. What many people at the time were hailing as a new genre of writing—autofiction or a sort of unclassifiable, cross-genre essay writing—Pitol had been doing for decades.

Discovering Pitol gave me the same rush as when I'd first read such universal writers as Cervantes and Dostoevsky, Virginia Woolf and Marcel Proust. There was something in the intellectual generousness of *The Art of Flight*, the easy knowledge bestowed to the reader with sympathy and grace. I knew immediately that Sergio Pitol was a universal writer.

Pitol is the universal writer par excellence: he was a translator, a professor, a diplomat, a cultural attaché, and a bit of a polymath. He was Mexican as well, though Pitol was Mexican the same way Shakespeare was English or Machado de Assis was Brazilian. Universal writers belong to all of us, and when we read them we wish to take them as our own. I can't say exactly what makes a writer a universal writer—only the reader knows—but in their capable hands, a universal writer illuminates timeless human truths, ideals and ideas which speak to us, touching us in a way nearly as intimate as our own inner voices; a universal writer engages the reader's sympathy—whether the reader is a bus driver in Trinidad or a housewife in Stockholm—by the accessible and democratic perspective in their work. Frequently, a universal writer writes about one specific place, and yet, in their hands, the place is beside the point, transformed into wherever you happen to be. As Daniel Saldaña París once wrote: "Pitol is a writer of another kind: his importance lies on the page, in the creation of his own world, in his ability to shed light on the world."

I say I "discovered" Pitol when, truthfully, I'd been watching Deep Vellum with a keen eye. Still a young press when Pitol was first published, hardly in its second year, Deep Vellum was committed to publishing international literature, a Quixotic mission to say the least. I was a bookseller in Houston, and Deep Vellum's home base of Dallas belonged to that other large sibling in the vast continent of Texas. In Texas things as idealistic as establishing a nonprofit publisher—focused on books in translation, no less—would certainly strike the traditionalist as a bit *uncanny*, even a touch *mad*. And yet, over a decade later, I find myself in the esteemed position of writing about Deep Vellum's *seventh* title by the great Sergio Pitol.

•

The Art of Flight was Sergio Pitol's first book to be translated into English and the first of a trilogy. And now we have the third book in *another* trilogy, *Married Life*. The three novels that make up the Carnival Triptych can be connected, but only in the most loose and casual way. A reader has no obligation to read a particular book before or after another, or be concerned with following the plot or a specific character.

The Love Parade is a historical detective novel which deftly connects a crime in Mexico City in 1942 with a historian in the 1980s who lived in the building as a young boy. Before long a colorful gallery of personalities emerge: dubious expats, melancholy detectives, busty matriarchs, eccentric twins, painters and sculptors. Pitol's characters, and by extension Pitol himself, aren't concerned so much with the world of commerce and politics (though their roles are invaluable in the backdrop) as much as art, literature, travel, what we enjoy calling "culture" and "society." Pitol's books are especially interested in the behavior of the people who inhabit this society as well as its myriad hierarchies. In *The Love Parade*, we're not simply given the art collector, for instance, but the gallerist as well as the artist themselves; each layer of community is explored with nimble and mischievous intelligence. When the procession of characters are paraded before the reader and start to gain dimension, the reader understands Pitol's achievement, as well as a rare look at the global effects of World War II on Mexico City.

In *Taming the Divine Heron*, Pitol turns a single evening into a comedy of outlandish proportion; the humor is scatological, the culture is cross-continental (Italy, Mexico, and Turkey); there's an obsession with Russian literature, travel fatigue, and siblings who test one's patience. Did I say a single evening? Perhaps I should say *two* evenings, since the evenings take place decades apart—the same way the simultaneous narrative in *Heart of Darkness* takes place on a ship in London and on a steamer in the African Congo years earlier.

Taming The Divine Heron is a cultural satire of gargantuan proportion, a brilliant comedy in the darkest and most satisfying way. Amidst a thunderstorm, a Mexico City family is held captive by, of all things, a story. The storyteller, our narrator, a bombastic, insufferable attorney named Dante C. de la Estrella, delves into the past to evoke a trip to Istanbul which he claims changed the course of his life and which introduces the reader to the eponymous "Heron" (yes, another insufferable, bombastic character). A dinner scene unfolds that's a monumental burlesque concerning a microscopic event. Egos. Language barriers. Misunderstandings writ large. Like Saul Bellow's *Humboldt's Gift*, it's a novel of big ideas and bad manners.

And now, finally, we have *Married Life*, where Pitol puts marriage, as well as class, culture, and infidelity under his deft microscope. An epiphany occurs to the protagonist, Jacqueline Cascorro, in the opening pages (while breaking a crab leg), and a novel of marriage, cousins, and cheating spouses unfolds. It's funny, sad, but, ultimately, it's *human*.

Each novel in the Carnival Triptych presents Pitol's singular view of humanity, our many faults and quirks, our voracious desire to be admired and understood—in short, our oh-so-human foibles. There's plenty to satirize, but just as much to love and forgive. Pitol's understanding and patience for our hare-brained species is infinite.

There are writers whose interest lies solely in language; others concerned by the subject itself; and others, rarer, concerned with both. This is Sergio Pitol. Diplomat. Humanist. World traveler. Mexican. Winner of the Cervantes Prize. A writer whose concerns lie in the realms of the sublime. Literature is what Pitol sought. Literature with a capital L. And not by preciousness or pretentiousness, but through an undying belief in the power of language. He was a Literature unto himself.

•

It often takes a unique convergence of circumstances for a book, any book, to be published. When great literature is published it feels like alchemy, a kind of rare magic: so many things work *against* the writer: our fickle and arbitrary tastes, shrinking attention spans, the political climate, bad taste and/or timing. (Did I mention money?) This is why certain writers feel like magicians and their books like magic tricks; from a cruel and pragmatic point of view, they probably *shouldn't* exist. As a North American reader, a *gringo* passionate for this magic, I feel indebted to George Henson and Deep Vellum for translating and publishing the work of Sergio Pitol. These books represent priceless gifts: of culture, of history, of a singular mind. But more than that, they represent the gift of literature itself, which is sublime and never-ending.

Translator's Note: My Marriage to Sergio Pitol

In her *Literary Hub* review of Michael F. Moore's translation of Alessandro Manzoni's *The Betrothed*, Pulitzer Prize-winning author and translator Jhumpa Lahiri observed:

> A translation also celebrates a union between author and translator, between the two languages they represent, and this connection, which feels sacred for many translators, endures even after the work of the translation has finished.
>
> The fruit of the union between an author and a translator is what enables literature to proliferate, perpetuate, and seduce readers around the world.

I titled this translator's note "My Marriage to Sergio Pitol" before reading Lahiri's review. What is this "sacred union," however, if not a marriage in literary form?

It is not mere coincidence that she and I have arrived at the same metaphor for similarly titled novels. As the only translator to have brought any of Pitol's books into English, to say I feel something akin to marriage is not just metaphorical. There certainly has been a union, the fruit of which has been seven translated books over the course of ten years, all midwifed by Deep Vellum.

To extend the metaphor, if Pitol and I were married, it would be a proxy marriage of sorts, such as the one between Clovis I King of the Franks and Clotilde in 496, or Pedro I of Brazil and Maria Leopoldina of Austria on 13 May 1817.

I say proxy marriage because Sergio Pitol and I never met. Our only interaction, in fact, was by way of a single, very cordial email, which read: "Your interest in my work fills me with happiness and gratitude. I would love nothing more than to see my Trilogy of Memory translated into English, a language that I adore and in which none of my books exists." After receiving this polite proposal, I decided it would be appropriate that I meet my future groom. So in 2013, during a summer trip to Havana, upon learning that Pitol was also in the Cuban capital, where he had traveled for treatments at a private clinic for the progressive primary aphasia that ultimately robbed him of language and his life, I attempted to meet him. An intermediary, our celestina (our matchmaker, that is), Miguel Barnet, offered to help arrange a meeting, a first look as it were. Alas, circumstances conspired against our meeting. (If this metaphor is sounding queerer and queerer—intended / offered in all its polysemy—think of it as a parody of a translator's note that Pitol might turn into a novel.)

I would attempt to meet my groom again two years later. During a trip to Mexico City, I offered to travel to Xalapa, the capital of the coastal state of Veracruz, where the Maestro lived. By this time, I was finishing my translation of *The Art of Flight*—his first book to appear in English—and had a myriad of questions—mostly about translation—that I wanted to (pro)pose to him. What, for example, did he mean by "la princesita negra de los brezos," which I'd later learn was a reference to a nineteenth-century German novel, *Das Heideprinzesschen* (1860) by Eugenie John, under the penname E.

Marlitt, which was translated into English as *The Princess of the Moor* in 1872 (I have been unable to track down the translator's name) and then into Spanish in 1896 as *La princesita de los brezos* (the translator of which is also unknown)?

As I mention in my translator's note to *The Art of Flight*, Pitol "modifies the title by adding the adjective *negra* (black) in order to describe an effeminate young black man of high rank whom he observes in a two-bit dive in Barcelona's gothic quarter." As I would soon learn, this use of arcane intertextuality was classic Pitol. This can be seen again when, in *Taming the Divine Heron*, he writes, "pues cargaban más enfermedades de las que cabrían en el pellejo de una rata," which could be translated in a variety of ways, but once the translator discovers—if they do, and I did—that Pitol is borrowing from Flann O'Brien's *The Third Policeman* (published by Dalkey Archive, now an imprint of Deep Vellum), in which the Irish novelist writes, "Because a man can have more disease and germination in his gob than you'll find in a rat's coat," you're obligated to translate "pellejo" as "coat" rather than "pelt" or "hide" or "hair" or "fur," all of which would, otherwise, be acceptable translations . . . if not for O'Brien.

As for *Married Life*, see if you can discover the hint of intertextuality that I believe Pitol has created in this last sentence of the first paragraph: "[S]e dejó poseer por un pensamiento que la visitaría de manera intermitente, convirtiéndola, y ya para siempre, en una mujer de muy malas ideas," which I translated as: "[S]he allowed herself to be possessed by a thought that was to visit her intermittently, transforming her, forever after, into a woman of very bad ideas."

If you guessed Dickens (see the allusion below), then I will consider my translation a success:

> Further, that it is the desire of the present possessor of that property, that he be immediately removed from his present sphere of life and from this place, and be brought up as a gentleman,—in a word, as a young fellow of great expectations.

It was that last phrase—"a young fellow of great expectations"—that I heard when I reached the end of *Married Life's* opening paragraph. Given Pitol's penchant for borrowing from the writers he read, I am convinced that the phrase, "a woman of very bad ideas," was indeed a nod to Dickens, who was one of Pitol's favorite authors, and whom he mentions seven times in *The Art of Flight*, twice in *The Journey*, and another seven times in *The Magician of Vienna*, where he singles out *Great Expectations*, writing:

> First readings are critical to the fate of a would-be writer. And he, years later, will discover the importance that those long hours held when he was obligated to forego thousands of celebrations to be alone with *Anna Karenina*, *The Charterhouse of Parma*, *Madame Bovary*, *Great Expectations*.

Worth noting, too, is his mention in *The Art of Flight* of another Dickens novel: "I should also cite the impulse born of a genre that I love, the comedy of errors, those by Tirso and Shakespeare, especially, and in the novel *Our Mutual Friend* by Dickens."

I include this last quote because *Married Life* is, as are *The Love Parade* and *Taming the Divine Heron*, a comedy of errors. How else to explain a woman who, during a failed attempt to murder her husband, loses two fingers? How can a reader not recognize the parody with which Pitol describes the tragicomic heroine (antiheroine?) Jacqueline?

> She felt dizzy, anxious, sad, she remembered that years before, when she still had all her fingers, a palm reader had told her that her emotional equilibrium would be disturbed in a serious way by the future absence of an index and middle fingers. Those weren't exactly the fingers that had been lost in the shooting, but no matter . . .

Whence Pitol's Penchant for Parody?

Our Cervantes laureate provides clues throughout his Trilogy of Memory—*The Art of Flight*, *The Journey*, and *The Magician of Vienna*. In *The Art of Flight*, when lauding Gabriel Vargas, the great Mexican cartoonist and creator of the comic strip *La Familia Burrón*, Pitol tells us: "My sense of parody, my play with the absurd, come from [Vargas] and not, as I would like to be able to boast, from Gogol or Gombrowicz." In *The Magician of Vienna*, however, he confesses: "As a tacit or explicit homage to some of my tutelary gods: Nikolai Gogol, H. Bustos Domecq, and Witold Gombrowicz, among others, I wrote *The Love Parade*, *Taming the Divine Heron*, and *Married Life*, a trilogy of novels closer to the carnival than any other rite." Among the "others" whom Pitol seems to downplay here is Russian literary theorist Mikhail Bakhtin, whose theory of the carnivalesque Pitol had discovered reading Baktin's *Rabelais and His World* (in Spanish: *La cultura popular en la Edad Media y en el Renacimiento*) during a period of convalescence in Marienbad in the mid-1980s.

From Trilogy to Triptych

After translating Pitol's Trilogy of Memory, followed by a collection of short stories titled *Mephisto's Waltz*, I began work on the three novels that Pitol would christen his Carnival Triptych—*Married Life* being the final novel. How exactly did this triptych come about? In *The Art of Flight*, the first volume of the Trilogy of Memory, Pitol tells us:

> [*The Love Parade*] was followed by another, *Married Life*, where in the very proper and measured language employed at the family dinner table when there are respected guests, I describe forty years of joyous marital breakdown. Shortly after finishing it, I discovered that *The Love Parade*, *Taming the Divine Heron*, and *Married Life* formed a natural triptych, without any preconceived idea. The function of the communicating vessels established between the three novels suddenly seemed clear: it tended to reinforce the grotesque vision that sustained them. Everything that aspired to solemnity, canonization, and self-satisfaction careened suddenly into mockery, vulgarity, and derision. A world of masks and disguises prevailed. Every situation, together as well as separate, exemplifies the three fundamental stages that Bakhtin finds in the carnivalesque farce: crowning, uncrowning, and the final scourging.

Finally, in *The Magician of Vienna*, he provides us with a key to reading *Married Life*:

> With *Married Life* the triptych comes to an end. A metaphorical tale about one of society's most well-worn institutions: marriage. The aim, if one can be clearly delineated, would be to demonstrate the obsolete structure of our institutions, the immense layer of colored stucco with which the so-called lifeblood, the powers that be, and the institutions masked reality until transforming it into a trap. If anything approaches a moral, it is the Gombrowiczian indication that the role of the writer and of the artist is to destroy those façades in order to allow what has been hidden for centuries to live. Between these three novels there exists a wide network of connections, of corridors, of vessels that strengthen their carnivalesque, farcical, hilarious, and grotesque character.

If you've read the first two volumes of the triptych—if you haven't, it's not too late—you know that Pitol has a fondness for the ribald, in keeping with the carnivalesque. How ribald? You might be surprised, perhaps even shocked, when you read how I've translated "la jamona con el rabo más verde que se haya visto en México," which you'll find midway through chapter one. (Hint: It appears in quotation marks.)

But wait, it gets worse (or better, depending on your tastes) and, not surprisingly, more difficult to translate. In the next chapter, Pitol transforms a rather harmless expression into a rather bawdy accusation against the wife on Jacqueline's lover Gaspar, writing, "Un buen día la encontrarían con la botica abierta y la pescuezona en la Puerta." Here Pitol is riffing on "la botica abierta y el boticario a la puerta" (literally: the drugstore open and the druggist at the door), which is a playful and harmless way of telling little boys that their fly is open. I originally translated it as, "One fine day they'd catch her with her skirt up and her panties down." After rereading the original, however, I felt that my translation not only strayed too far from the original, it also omitted an important element: the "boticario" (druggist), which Pitol replaces with "pescuezona," from the word "pescuezo" (neck, usually of an animal), which here, by way of a rather vulgar metonymy (or is it synecdoche?), based on appearance (the augmentative suffix "-ona" suggests a large size), to refer to a penis. (Interestingly, the noun is feminine, but considering other vulgarisms for penis—"verga," "pinga," "polla"—are also feminine, the gender here suggests that the inference is correct.)

How to solve, or resolve, this translation puzzle? I thought and I thought and I thought, then I thought some more. After all, translation is often just that. Solution after solution turned out not to be the solution. Ultimately—don't ask me how, my thought process is a mystery even to me—it occurred to me to riff on the idiom "rooster in the henhouse." So I offered my editor an option: the aforementioned translation or "One fine day they'd find the door to the henhouse open and the rooster inside." Which one made it? You'll have to continue to read to find out. Honestly, I don't know which Pitol would prefer. I do know, as only a spouse would know, that he was a fan of free translation.

This admittedly vexing idiom aside, I'd be lying if I said that *Married Life* was the easiest of the seven Pitol books I've translated. After all, it would be natural to assume that by number seven, Pitol's prose and I have grown to know each other intimately. And, yes, that's true, to a certain extent. But even in his shortest novel, at just under thirty-two thousand words, we find the long, labyrinthine sentences, such as this 124-word sentence, punctuated with staccato-like parentheticals, that are Pitol's trademark and which I labored to keep intact:

> One rainy afternoon, in the scant and impersonal apartment occupied by David Carranza in Colonia Condesa, after fornicating freely and pleasurably, Jacqueline, in a state of obvious exaltation, assured him that his misfortunes arose from the fact that he was too noble, that nothing in his person concealed his greatness, which surely aroused the envy and resentment of that foul pack of resentful, frustrated, middling social climbers who surrounded him, which Carranza accepted with a vague lack of conviction; he needed, she added, capital to back him so that he could embark on the realization of his dreams on a grand scale, not squander his talents being someone's secretary; to have at his disposal a newspaper, for example, that could help enhance his personality.

From the Ribald to the Mundane

As usual, I have left most place names and other toponyms (Monumento de la Revolución, Colonia Condesa) and odonyms (Calle Orizaba, Avenida Ribera de San Cosme) in Spanish. While I am still a fervent proponent of foreignization, this novel, more than the two previous ones, lends itself to what translation theorists call a "target language bias," that is, a translation strategy that favors the structure and idioms of the target rather than the source text. I view the bias toward the target language to be a result rather than a strategy, however. Plainly put, years of reading and translating English prose—Pitol translated seven Henry James novels—have, in my opinion, greatly influenced Pitol's prose. That said, surely I will be criticized, as some have done in the past, for sentences like "She slurred her words, as if pronouncing them cost her great effort," being distractingly close to the Spanish. This I wear as a badge of honor.

Foreignization by Any Other Name

As I reread my translation to find elements that I thought worthy of mention in this note, I asked myself why I choose to translate "sangre fría" (cold blood) as "sangfroid" in the following sentence: "Jacqueline recibió la información de que Gaspar seguía trabajando al lado de su marido con una sangre fría que ella misma calificó de admirable y que desconcertó por entero a su hermana." ("Jacqueline received the information that Gaspar continued to work at her husband's side with a sangfroid that she herself described as admirable and which confounded her sister entirely.") Perhaps because Jacqueline, whose first name is already French, began to pronounce her last name as if it too were French: "She didn't change her last name because such an act would have offended her parents, but she began to pronounce it as if it were French: Cascorró. Jacqueline Cascorró!"

In that same vein, why did I translate "madre mía," not as "my goodness," or something equally formulaic, but as "mamma mia"? Perhaps I was listening to ABBA at the time, but more likely it was because the character who speaks it, a certain Gianni Ferraris, was "a young man of Italian extraction" who was hired to lecture "on the high points of art history" every Tuesday and Thursday in classes Jacqueline attended at the home of Márgara

Armengol in Coyoacán. Whatever the reason, I have the feeling Pitol, whose four grandparents were Italian immigrants, and who held until his death an abiding love for all things Italian, would approve.

And perhaps Lahiri, who writes in, and translates to and from, Italian might too.

Grazie mille, maestro. It has been one heck of a marriage!

G.B. Henson
Pacific Grove, California
2025

CHAPTER 1

JACQUELINE CASCORRO, THE PROTAGONIST OF this story, knew during the better part of her life the everyday experiences of marriage: ecstasies, squabbles, infidelities, crises, and reconciliations. Everything changed in an instant when, as she broke a crab leg with her hands and heard the popping of a champagne cork behind her, she allowed herself to be possessed by a thought that was to visit her intermittently, transforming her, forever after, into a woman of very bad ideas.

For years, a blue notebook accompanied her on the various moves through which her troubled wedded life had taken her, without her being aware of its existence; it was a very thin notebook, fastened with a rubber band to a collection of notes on literature and art history, deposited at the bottom of an ornately decorated box, which she acquired in Pátzcuaro during her honeymoon. The box remains in the cellar at L'Aiglon, a restaurant in Cuernavaca, where Jacqueline left almost the entirety of her household effects when she decided to move to Veracruz. She would surely be astonished if she were to read the literary passages copied many years ago in that long-forgotten notebook. She would, make no mistake, with melancholy, pine for the intellectual labor that nourished the noblest, purest part of her being, the only one that for a time offered her any kind of security, destroyed completely by the violence that upended her life with unbounded scandal. Because from a given moment it was no longer possible for her to possess any illusions in that regard: her spiritual life was shattered.

Jacqueline had used two pages in the notebook to copy the literary passages that interested her and another to express her feelings about what she considered her marital failure; the rest had been left blank. It wasn't difficult to see that those notes had been written during a period of intense bitterness, during one of the initial crises of her marriage, before she'd resigned herself to accept her husband's infidelities as inevitable. Alicia Villalba—Nicolás Lobato's cousin of modest means who worked as his secretary—as well as other female employees, kept her informed day to day about the activities of her unfaithful husband. They'd spend hours on end glued to the phone to describe the raffishness of a fake blonde with whom Nicolás locked himself in room number seventeen, specifying: on the third floor—as if the floor number were of any importance!—of the Eslavia Hotel, located on Calle Orizaba, as it was rare that he set foot in the Asunción, much less to celebrate his erotic escapades, considering it perhaps beneath his status. The truth was that soon after her marriage, Jacqueline had learned not to suffer like a hysterical madwoman, which in no way implied that she approved of Nicolás Lobato's dissolute life. A chance reading of a few pages of Balzac's *Physiology of Marriage* led her to the conclusion that most women, a few years after marrying, only experience a deep aversion, an almost absolute repulsion, towards their husbands: a common result of the tyranny to which they have been so arbitrarily subjected.

The first thing she copied into the blue notebook was this

categorical statement from the French text: *The bed is the whole of marriage*. She punctuated the sentence with three or four exclamation points, then crossed the sentence out in a fit of rage and, accordingly, the exclamation points she'd added.

She then wrote in green ink that life is fueled by passion and that no passion can survive marriage.

Also, that marriage is an institution necessary for the maintenance of societies, but that, however (and there she added in parentheses the exclamation: *hélas!*), the institution is contrary to the laws of Nature, that a married woman is treated like a slave, that there are no completely blissful marriages, that marriage is fraught with crimes, and that the murders that are discovered aren't the worst. She drew several lines in different colors of ink under this last statement, as if she'd already glimpsed the flutter of premonition.

Abandoned in a cellar in Cuernavaca whence she'd never recover it, the blue notebook in which she wrote these and other literary quotations had disappeared from her memory several years before she traveled to Veracruz. The circumstances in which those lines were written had become even more blurry. If someone had come to ask her when and with whom she'd been unfaithful to her husband for the first time, she'd have answered, without the slightest shadow of a doubt, that her first lover had been Gaspar Rivero, a contemptible louse whom she'd helped in the most selfless way, only to be stabbed in the back in return, and that it happened shortly before he started working at the Asunción—a hotel lacking any charm located a stone's throw from the Monumento de la Revolución—with no memory at all of her true pioneer: an engineer from Guanajuato, whom she'd met at a party at Márgara Armengol's home. The entire episode had faded from her memory. If, after putting her to sleep, a doctor or a hypnotist had asked her a question about it, she might have been able to recall that at a certain point a man who was beginning to leave his youth behind was introduced to her at a party and she invited him, out of mere courtesy, to sit next to her; she'd by then drunk a couple of stiff Cuba libres and begun to tell that perfect stranger that a distinguished professor of philosophy had recently acknowledged in that very house that she was endowed with the most exquisite sensitivity he'd encountered in his long professional career. To the point of citing her as an example to a group of envious dilettantes who might have anything but that, sensitivity, and straightaway explained to the man from Guanajuato how hard she had to fight to preserve that refined gift from the low blows inflicted on her by the brutal man who was her husband, a barbarian who'd reduced his life's interests to mere money, mere lust.

"No matter how much anyone may argue to the contrary, I'm convinced that no one will ever be able to guess what a person can become over the years," she murmured in a confidential tone to the stranger. "I'd never have been able to guess that the Nicolás Lobato I met, the one who later became my husband—don't apologize, you've no reason to know him, he's not anyone who's excelled in any way—would become what he is now. We used to meet in the afternoons at the café at the Casa de los Mascarones. Do you know it?"

"Who?" asked the man, who'd paid little attention to her words.

"No one. I'm referring to the café at the Mascarones; it was inside the Faculty of Philosophy and Letters, that is, when it was still located on Avenida Ribera de San Cosme. A beautiful place; those of us who frequented it in our university days still feel like orphans. I met Nicolás Lobato in that café. He doesn't like people to know. I don't know why, considering he's now involved in other activities, but neither of us managed to finish our studies. Nicolás was studying political science. He spent his afternoons in a fleapit on Calle Miguel Schultz, just around the corner from Philosophy and Letters. I went there several times to pick him up; it was a run-down two-story dump of a house that no one would ever have imagined could be home to a university faculty. What a difference from my faculty! As different as heaven and earth, between my husband and yours truly, if you'll forgive my lack of modesty." She let out a brief chortle. "Nicolás showed up almost every afternoon at Mascarones. He took a geography class in the faculty, and I don't know what else, a language I think, most likely English. I'm convinced that he doesn't even remember what he was studying at the time. He was always careless and lackadaisical about his studies. He spent most of his time at the café; that's how we met. We used to take the same streetcar in the evenings. Or rather two, because there wasn't a direct line that would take me home. He'd get off at Eugenia, in Colonia del Valle, and I'd go on to Coyoacán. Sometimes Márgara would be with us. That's when our friendship began. We lived very close to one another. I lived on Calle Berlín, just around the corner from the house she's never left. Ours was a beautiful property," she declared with a tone laden with nostalgia. "We never quite managed to escape the walls that surrounded our childhood. When I got married, my mother, a widow with all her daughters married off, moved to an apartment in Colonia Narvarte. What was the poor thing going to do in that rambling old house? Nicolás was an only child; as a boy he always sprained his ankles when he walked. That detail, according to Alicia Villalba, his cousin, a woman who dresses like a man, necktie and all, explains much of his behavior. We must have been dating for about a semester when his father fell ill, which obliged him to take over the hardware store, downtown, on Calle de Mesones, which he inherited soon after. He clung to that lifeline to justify dropping out of university when the truth was that he couldn't take life as a student anymore. He was madly in love with me, I must admit, so even though he no longer went to the faculty, we continued to see each other rather frequently. I also acknowledge that during our courtship he never exerted any undue pressure on me, such that I was able to arrive at the altar a virgin, which in those days—I assure you—still held considerable cachet. When his father died, he left him the hardware store and a tidy sum of money, which allowed him to channel his assets into hotels. He sold the hardware store, which was the right decision because he couldn't take it anymore. He could finally breathe. I'm sure he was forced to engage in all kinds of funny business because he was able to get his hands on some dead and dying hotels for a few measly pesos. His first acquisition was the Asunción, a purchase he always regretted: a seedy, rundown hotel located between the Monumento de la Revolución and Paseo de la Reforma, which from day one inspired nothing but disappointment; then the one on Calle Orizaba, the much nicer Eslavia. Ever since then, he hasn't thought of anything but building a huge hotel in Cuernavaca, that's his obsession, that and, more than any other, women." She paused briefly to take a drink; when she saw that her neighbor, whom she'd condemned to silence, was about to get up, she put a hand on his thigh to stop him and continued: "Don't worry, I'm not going to beleaguer you by recounting the tribulations of my married life. Look, if there's one thing I love in life, it's coming to Márgara's home on Saturdays. More than just university friends, we've been sisters from the start. I love the atmosphere that runs through this house. Pure culture! Deep down we all have something of the bohemian in us, don't you agree? I'm like a fish in water here. As you've probably seen, I've done everything in my power to keep my spirit alive. It's always difficult for a man to understand what it means for a woman to be able to cultivate herself," and without remembering that a moment earlier she'd spoken of the spacious home where she spent her childhood, she continued: "It's unseemly that I'm telling you this, but growing up there were five of us kids—three girls and two boys—and until I got married all three girls had to share a single room: María Dorotea, María del Carmen, and me, who still went by a frightful name back then. How was I supposed to read in those conditions? When was I supposed to study for my exams? With a lousy sixty-volt bulb, to boot! Where was I supposed to get the money to buy the required books? I did what I could! And much more, I dare say! Cheers! As I told you, the only thing Nicolás Lobato thinks about is money and lust. We were really young when we got married. In a way I was still a child on my wedding day. I could never have foreseen what awaited me. Except for Alicia Villalba, who is really, I mean really, masculine, Nicolás hasn't forgiven any of the women who work in his businesses, all of whom, if you'll pardon the expression, he's got to shake the sheets at least once. He treats them like whores, just as he'd like to treat me." A waiter passed with a tray of drinks, and she took another Cuba libre, and continued to talk about her marital vicissitudes, only to discover at a certain point that the guy to whom she'd confided so many intimacies was no longer beside her, that she'd been talking instead to a couple of teenagers who were playing at putting on and taking off a blonde wig that'd seen better days, and ended up sticking it on her head as if it were a helmet; they asked her the most salacious questions imaginable and laughed at her confused and bashful answers; they told her, amid guffaws, appalling aspects of the sexual life of a certain Cuquita—"a piece of skirt with the ripest ass Mexico's ever seen"—a phrase they added every time they mentioned her, whom she neither knew nor cared to know, celebrating with bursts of laughter every new profanity they spouted, such that at a certain point she felt obliged to stand up and shout that they were a couple of snotnosed morons, that they didn't know with whom they had the honor of speaking, and that in case they hadn't realized it, she'd take the liberty to announce that they were dealing with a lady that night, that they were talking... and there she drew a blank, looked around, saw a number of faces, not only those of the pair of impertinent boys, who were looking at her with amused expectation, and finished her rodomontade as best she could...repeating that they were indeed talking to a lady, to a lady who'd suffered much in life and who therefore deserved to be treated better than her husband did, an Attila in the fullest sense of the word, who'd run off to Cuernavaca on weekends to bang his female employees or the first bimbos who came along... The pair of boys burst out laughing again and both, almost in unison, told her not to be so stupid and to stop playing the martyr. Did she perhaps find her husband inadequate after those orgiastic weekends? Surely not; the most eminent sexologists affirmed that a man's penis, more than that of other animals, was like a soap that was never used up; on the contrary, the more use it got the better job it did. She got up once again because she thought they were disrespecting her, plain and simple, and because of her esteem for Márgara Armengol she couldn't allow herself to make the scene in her home she was itching to. When she went into the other room, she discovered that there were very few guests left. Suddenly, Márgara was at her side asking her if she was feeling okay, if by chance one of the drinks hadn't sat well with her, as several guests had confessed to feeling unwell, attributing it to the quality of the alcohol, which Jacqueline considered a rather indiscreet detail on the part of the hostess, since it had been she who'd brought the drinks that night, but like a true lady she said nothing; then the hostess suggested that it might be appropriate to have someone drive her home, or, if she preferred, she could wait a little while until the gathering was over and stay overnight in the studio. She wouldn't allow her to leave by herself—absolutely not!—as it was clear that she was drowned in her cups. At that moment the guest to whom she'd recounted the many inconveniences of being Nicolás Lobato's wife reappeared, and at Márgara's request, said yes, he'd be happy to accompany her home, although if he took her anywhere, it would be to the apartment of a friend, since he was from Guanajuato and didn't have a place in Mexico City. She saw this person, whose name she never seemed to recall, a couple of times more at Márgara's parties, and at the end of both the same thing occurred. The last time she was in the apartment, as she was telling the Guanajuato native in detail what kind of lovers her husband preferred, he went to a bookshelf, removed Balzac's *Physiology of Marriage* and put it in her hands, telling her it was a gift, which to her seemed as unseemly as Márgara's comments about the alcohol, since that apartment, and hence everything in it, books included, didn't belong to him.

Whether that man returned later to Guanajuato, she neither knew nor cared. And if Jacqueline saw him on another occasion, she must have greeted him with an indifference bordering on boorishness, which wasn't an obstacle to her talking to him with furious incoherence in that borrowed apartment where she spent the night on three occasions about the time Alicia Villalba—her husband's cousin and secretary—phoned her shortly after their marriage to tell her that Nicolás wouldn't be coming home that weekend because he had to go take a look at some parcels of land that were for sale in Cuernavaca, adding that he'd tried on several occasions to contact but was unable to reach her, so he'd given her the task of informing her of his departure, only to add a moment later that Nicolás had invited a new employee who dyed her rather dirty hair with a carrot-colored dye and who was wearing purple stockings like those that the cheapest prostitutes wear, and from that moment on she, who'd come to the marriage as a virgin, knew that she wasn't the only woman in her husband's bed; this is why when Nicolás would march off to Cuernavaca she'd attend, as compensation, the cultural get-togethers at Márgara Armengol's home, to hear people discuss books, theater, cinema, and not just talk about business as was the case of late at home. As for the man from Guanajuato: she never remembered his name or his build, so it was impossible for her to consider him her lover. Even when he was, while she was under his body, shuddering from apparent bursts of passion, and he ran his tongue along her thighs or lay siege to her nipples with delicate nibbles, she continued to recount how Nicolás Lobato tried to brutalize her, how he'd tried unsuccessfully to destroy her sensitivity, thanks to the sustenance she received from people of a higher status who frequented those Saturday nights, and that if it were up to her, she'd live her whole life in the company of Márgara and her refined friends, although it must be said that of late certain young vulgarians had snuck into her home, which was regrettable, to take liberties as soon as they discovered a woman alone, with no one there to defend her. So in order to remain close to Márgara, she made living in Coyoacán a condition when she was asked in marriage, and Nicolás agreed even though, curiously enough, he didn't seem to consider her friend to be a person, just as when they were students and the three of them had to travel on the same streetcar to return home.

Jacqueline had become a walking disaster. Were it not for her providing the most necessary elements to hold these weekly meetings, she'd never have been invited again. She spent several years telling Márgara Armengol's friends, who came to fear her like the plague, and to avoid her as much as possible, how her husband brutalized her, how men in general bored her, and sometimes even life itself, with the exception of books, paintings, music, theater, flowers, the always intelligent conversation with Márgara, her university companion, her neighbor, more a sister than a friend, and the select group with which she'd been able to surround herself. That was, she maintained, opening her plump arms and waving them eloquently, the only world she could truly consider her own, the only one, too, where he could feel at ease. Márgara always imposed on one of her guests, as a special favor, to take care of her. From time to time, Jacqueline would visit bookstores and buy three or four new releases. She scarcely managed to leaf through them, read the front and back covers, and convince herself that this was contributing to her ongoing edification.

Six or seven years passed in this way. To the two hotels, Nicolás had added a travel agency on Calle Londres, which had turned out to be a gold mine, but didn't result in a change of any kind in Jacqueline's life. The change—and on what scale!—came the day she arrived home to find Adrián, her younger brother, in her living room. He was a layabout, a waste of space, a freeloader, who in recent times had been trying to make a living by publishing the occasional lackluster article in a working-class evening paper; since adolescence she'd regarded her brother Adrián as a high-handed, overfamiliar mooch, a disastrous combination by any reckoning. In as dry a tone as possible she asked him why he'd shown up at her home unannounced, and at that very moment she noticed another young man in the living room, dressed almost identically to her brother, in a gray double-breasted pinstripe suit. Both instantly rose to their feet. In any event, Adrián was preferable to Marcelo, their older brother, whose baleful, dissembling air repulsed her. Adrián was unable to write anything but fluff, but it must be said that between a journalist and a worker at a flea market there was a vast difference. Marcelo's appearance, not to mention his wife's, whose name she could never remember, was slatternly and repulsive. The only virtue she could find in him was that he never showed up at her home at mealtime, and that he wasn't a freeloader: he'd never tried to get money out of her or Nicolás. Moreover, he seemed to have no desire to see them regularly.

"I'm positive you have no idea who this is," said Adrián jovially, pointing to the other young man, apparently oblivious to the cold reception. "Take a good look at 'im, guess, I bet you won't get it right. Give up? Yes, yes? It's none other than Gaspar Rivero, one of our cousins from Orizaba." The authoritarian scene she'd been about to stage suddenly froze. Cousin Gaspar greeted Jacqueline dutifully, but not obsequiously, and added that it would be difficult for her to remember him, since the time she and her parents passed through Orizaba on their way to Veracruz, he was so shy that when he saw them, he ran from the room for fear of being forced to open his mouth.

"I've never heard a voice like his, so unsettling," she confided to Márgara the next day. "Do you think it's possible to fall in love with a voice? I felt as if it were destined only to me. I don't know how to describe it to you; the only thing I can tell you is that no other voice has ever produced such emotion in me."

"Is he also interested in literature?"

"To tell you the truth, I wasn't able to pay attention to what he was saying. Apart from the first few sentences, I don't even know what he was talking about."

When Márgara asked her the usual questions, she couldn't say whether he was physically attractive or not; she did manage with some effort to remember that he was thin; she wasn't sure about his height; he wasn't short, perhaps medium height, she ventured, like her brother Adrián; she remembered instead that his face was angular, that his skin was somewhat neglected, his cheekbones too pronounced, and his eyelashes long and drooped to the point of almost covering his eyes.

Anyway, the day before, the day of the meeting, upon hearing her cousin talk about his shyness and fear of strangers, she smiled benevolently. She was waiting for Adrián to give her an explanation about his presence and that of his relative at her home. As the silence drew out, she decided to be the one to speak. She asked them to sit down and offered them a drink. Her husband would be home in half an hour at the latest, she specified; they would eat immediately, because he returned to the agency in the afternoons. In the meantime, Jacqueline learned the purpose of her brother's visit, and for the first time in a long while, she didn't send him packing. So great was the change that she went so far as to invite both young men to lunch. Adrián decided to clarify that he wanted to introduce Gaspar, the forgotten cousin from Orizaba, to Nicolás. Gaspar had lived in Mexico City years before and had taken some courses at a tourism school, without finishing them; in the last few years he'd worked in several hotels in Veracruz. He'd been in the capital for several weeks and was looking for a way to continue his studies, but he didn't have a job. Who else could one turn to in such cases if not to relatives? Gaspar had looked for him and finally found him. Knowing his situation and his experience in hotel matters, he thought that perhaps Nicolás would be interested in the services of a person in whom he could place all his trust.

"If your husband will listen to anyone, it's you, María Magdalena," Adrián commented.

"Jacqueline, although the pronunciation may prove difficult for you!" she answered curtly. And in the half hour of great confusion that followed she felt obliged to ask about her mother and sisters, whom she hadn't seen for some time, even though like a good daughter she sent her mother a check every month with the chauffeur, and continued to inquire about her brother Marcelo, her sisters, brothers-in-law and nephews, and, to show her cordiality, she also asked her cousin for news of his family, whom she didn't remember at all. Adrián was surprised by the sudden humanity he saw flowering in his sister. And in the face of this outpouring of goodwill, he confessed that he'd take advantage of the opportunity to try to obtain a loan from his brother-in-law, by no means an excessive amount, that would allow him to pay off pressing debts. He wasn't asking for a gift, he wanted that to be clear. He'd find a way to pay him with advertising for his hotels and his travel agency in the newspaper where he worked.

"When you know how to approach him, your husband can be quite a generous man," he continued, "the obstacle's always been you. When someone approaches Nicolás with a request, the answer is always the same: 'Talk to my wife first, and then we'll work out the details!' And everything ends there!"

She was dumbfounded that her brother dared to bare his heart in such a way. An hour later they were sitting at the table. Nicolás exuded happiness in those days. Everything in his life seemed to be moving toward perfection. He'd just acquired a very large parcel of land on the outskirts of Cuernavaca, a palm grove; he'd pursued it for months, resolved cumbersome legal difficulties over property rights, and at last the palm grove was his. He planned to create a one-of-a-kind tourist complex in the region. It was a cheerful lunch. Jacqueline snuck a look at her reflection in the buffet mirror. How fortunate that the day before she'd gone to the beauty salon! Maybe it was a premonition! Could it be true what the hairdresser had told her about her hair? That it looked thinner every day? She didn't believe it. That woman was confused, accustomed as she was to dealing with the bristly hair that most Mexican women have; hers was too delicate; angel hair, her father used to tell her when she was a child. In any case, she'd done her hair well. She was aware of the sidelong glances with which her cousin studied her. She thought, however, that she should submit herself to a light diet. She contemplated with disgust her small neck, wider than what was desirable; her broad Roman emperor-like face would benefit from an overall weight loss. She'd exercise. She'd be disciplined, consistent this time, for sure. Yes, yes, yes! she told herself with marked distrust; but the sparkle in her eyes, her smooth, delicate skin, her sparkling smile, made up for the other shortcomings. She was more than confident that she could compete with the women her cousin would've met in Orizaba and even with those in Veracruz. Her weight wasn't anything to despair about either. Starting the next day, she'd exercise. She participated in the conversation with exuberance; she talked about the way she'd behave when she became the queen of the hotel empire whose headquarters would be located in Cuernavaca. Everyone celebrated her witty remarks. Nicolás Lobato was surprised by her jovial tone, which had been absent for quite some time at home, and he thought it necessary to invite his wife's relatives more often in order to have the opportunity to enjoy her rejuvenation and forget the weary, tense, and complaining tenor that characterized their usual conversations.

As if she'd read her husband's mind, and after a sudden spell of euphoria, Jacqueline unexpectedly plunged into sadness. She contemplated the pinstripe suits of Adrián and her cousin, the ordinariness of the fabric, the inelegance of the cut, suits surely bought at a third-rate store; she compared them with the splendid cashmere and perfect cut of her husband's clothes. She remembered her childhood, life on a dead-end street in Coyoacán that was all but a tenement courtyard, a long alleyway with a dozen tiny shacks on either side, the daily despair. She thought of her mother, a dentist, attending to a handful of clients in a dingy office because she'd always lacked the money necessary to acquire the necessary equipment; of her father's emphysema, a middling employee at the Ministry of Public Education, whose illness grew increasingly painful and nightmarish in the months immediately before his death; of life at the edge of penury, a tiny room for her, María Dorotea, and María del Carmen, the cosmetics they shared, the lack of stockings, the want for winter clothes, for so many other things, for food no less, and she felt like bursting into tears. That she'd escaped from that hell was a source of pride; she'd made the decision, despite all imaginable obstacles, to enroll in the university, to change before marriage the much-hated name of María Magdalena Cascorro, with which she'd been christened, for that of Jacqueline, which gave her more self-confidence and served as compensation for all the shit she'd been forced to swallow. She didn't change her last name because such an act would have offended her parents, but she began to pronounce it as if it were French: Cascorró. Jacqueline Cascorró! And this inner recounting of old tribulations made her feel more sympathy for this young man who suddenly appeared in her life, who, she had no doubt, had known an existence similar to hers, and was determined to leave it behind. She turned to look at herself in the mirror, discovered the profound desolation that marked her face—surely a result of the flood of bad memories—and observed the three men who were conversing with such liveliness; it occurred to her that perhaps the only one capable of sensing her moods, of appreciating her sensitivity, was that cousin who'd just appeared, and she resolved to help him. As soon as the coffee was served, she'd attack the fortress. She would become a flaming angel, a fierce lioness, and a munificent princess. Gaspar would get a job, perhaps managing one of the hotels, or a position at the travel agency, anything, of course, that had nothing to do with Cuernavaca's new tourism project.

She was surprised by the boldness of her thoughts.

As she'd expected, it wasn't difficult to convince her husband to employ Gaspar, and an intimate relationship was established between the two cousins. For Jacqueline, life became more intense and colorful, her marriage flourished. She visited Márgara Armengol's home less, and the few times she did attend her gatherings she didn't bother the guests with the hackneyed story of an exquisite flower sullied by the mouth of a brutal, enuretic, and tyrannical husband.

Everything was going well until the moment when, as she broke a crab leg with her hands and heard the popping of a champagne cork behind her, she allowed herself to be possessed by a wicked thought. It was as if a flash of lightning were running through her, charging her with energy: her eyes sparkled, her hands trembled, her heart beat wildly. And that thought was to visit her intermittently, for the rest of her life, transforming her, forever after, into a woman not only of bad, but of disastrous ideas.

CHAPTER 2

NICOLÁS LOBATO ALLOWED SEVERAL DAYS to pass before deciding where to place his wife's cousin. Where he could really use him was at the new property he'd purchased near Cuernavaca. He needed someone there to supervise the project he was about to start, the ambitious complex he would call Las Palmas: hotel, swimming pools, bungalows, stables, tennis courts, and golf course. In a few weeks the land would be cleared. Then construction would begin. He'd be up to his neck in debt; he didn't care; in a matter of three or four years, if everything went according to plan, he'd be able to boast of owning one of the most magnificent resorts in the country. Jacqueline opposed her cousin's exile. The construction they were going to undertake was of an enormous scale, she said; it would be necessary to collateralize what they already owned in order to be able to finance the start-up, development, and completion of such a costly enterprise and at the same time allow them to live comfortably until Las Palmas began to make a profit. Why not give Gaspar a job in the ghastly Asunción? Perhaps he'd be able to sort out the management he'd distrusted from the moment he acquired the property. He could keep a close eye on that manager who'd made such a bad impression on him from the start. For Las Palmas, someone from Cuernavaca who was familiar with the lay of the land and the people would be more convenient. These arguments, not at all insignificant, earned Gaspar Rivero, for the time being, the position of manager of the Asunción Hotel restaurant, with the task of monitoring, to the extent possible, the management and operation of the hotel.

But here we should return to that wicked thought that troubled Jacqueline's mind, which was alluded to in the previous chapter. These bad ideas appeared like a searing flash on the twenty-third of April, nineteen hundred and sixty, during the celebration of her seventh wedding anniversary. She was, at the time, about to turn thirty. The party was held in an outdoor restaurant in Tlalpan. About two hundred people attended. Jacqueline noticed the change that was taking place in her husband's life from the very moment Alicia Villalba showed her the list of people invited to the reception: politicians, bankers, hoteliers and restauranteurs, society people, as well as some film actors and actresses to minimize the solemnity out of the festivities. Everything went perfectly. Jacqueline was impressed by the ease and naturalness with which her husband mingled with people she only knew from the society pages. Nicolás behaved as if he'd gone to school with them and had never stopped interacting with them. A pat of the back here, kisses on the women's cheeks there, smiles for everyone. Despite herself, she admired the penetrating sparkle of his teeth and the thick mustache he'd cultivated over the past few months. Nicolás, it was evident, wasn't celebrating another wedding anniversary but his entry into the social circle that he'd decided to join in order to launch the Las Palmas project. She was overcome with very mixed feelings; on the one hand, the pride that this brilliant man was her husband and the certainty that success would always accompany his ventures; on the other, an undeniable resentment for his having marginalized her from this new and splendid life, while she told herself, as if she had to make some sort of amends, that it was a hollow, fake existence, a mere façade, in no way comparable with the intense emotional life she secretly led, nor with the intellectual stimulation that Márgara Armengol's circle had offered her in the past. To avoid any weakness in response to Nicolás's new lifestyle, she had to remind herself that he was precisely the enemy against whom she had to defend herself, the person she had to defeat. She observed that Márgara and her friends weren't at all out of place in that setting; at their table one might sense a perhaps excessive, but still elegant, touch of eccentricity, a contrast that went well with the rest of the attendees. On the other hand, the incongruity of the two tables located at the back of the garden, specifically at the entrance to the kitchen, with the rest of the guests could not have been more pronounced. One of them was occupied by her mother, who'd agreed, as a special favor, to attend, and by María Dorotea, María del Carmen, their husbands, and her brother Adrián; Marcelo, flatly, wasn't invited. In the middle of that group, surely bored to death, sat Gaspar Rivero. If her brothers-in-law's clothes were deplorable, her sisters' attire was beyond comment: black satin dresses, round like balloons, down to their ankles, cuffs and collars of green lace, short jackets, also black, studded with green chintzy costume jewelry, possibly rented satin hats, with plumes of artificial bottle-green feathers rushing to one side of the face. Thus were they dressed. Her cousin's presence in the midst of that outlandish group exerted such a powerful magnetism on Jacqueline that she couldn't take her eyes off the table for more than five minutes. When she looked that direction, who she really saw was Gaspar Rivero. In her eyes, her sisters, her brothers-in-law, her brother Adrián, even her poor, beloved mother, made up a raucous and garishly colorful fauna that at first glance one might compare to a tree full of macaws. At the neighboring table sat Nicolás's trusted employees. Despite wearing a suit with an unduly masculine cut, Alicia Villalba was the height of elegance next to that motley crew of lowlife rabble, without the slightest knack for mingling and chatting with the rest of the guests.

There was a moment when she managed to react. She forced herself to look away from her cousin and circulate among the different groups with the same ease as her husband. She knew herself to be a woman of clever wit and ready smile; she was aware that she'd refined her resources at Márgara Armengol's Saturday socials. She sauntered through the garden, saying hello left and right, until managing to join her husband. She noticed that some women made no attempt to disguise a wry smile or a sneer as they greeted her. Jacqueline was undeterred. What that meant, and Márgara had already explained it to her on more than one occasion, was that she had a personality of her own, not subject to any trend, a way of being that took pleasure in dressing up, not putting on a uniform as was the case with most women, for which she wasn't easily forgiven. A few days before, when Alicia Villalba came by her house to deliver the invitations for her friends, she'd told her—very much in passing, as if to play it down—that Nicolás was looking for someone, an etiquette teacher, who could advise her on the best way to present herself in public. She was on the verge of bursting out laughing as she remembered that foolish remark, when suddenly, seeing herself full-length in front of a mirror, she pondered whether perhaps she'd been too bold to make her entrance that day in transparent plastic mules with fluorescent heels. Such divine accessories, she pondered dispassionately, were too avant-garde for Mexican society, which as a rule was very conservative.

As the last guests were leaving, the group of intimates, which had been seated at the tables next to the kitchen doors—that is, the family and the employees—went to the Lobatos' home. There, before going out, Jacqueline had put on a few bottles of champagne to chill and gave orders for some trays of sandwiches to be prepared. Alicia Villalba offered to take Jacqueline's mother to her apartment in Colonia Narvarte. The others left the restaurant en masse, cheering the Lobatos, eager to enjoy round two of the celebration. Her relatives had become a veritable cross to bear; it was impossible to say how much of a sacrifice it was to take that raucous and motley crew with her everywhere she went! She feared that her nerves wouldn't be able to withstand the torture, and when least expected she'd suffer an attack of hysteria. She was doing everything possible to prevent that from happening. The insinuations, the crude remarks from that band of deadbeats, who delighted in calling her María Magdalena at the top of their lungs, without regard for whether there were other people present, the constant requests for money from Adrián and her sisters, the familiarities, the abuses, she accepted everything so that her relationship with Gaspar Rivero, whose lover she'd been for some ten months, would disappear into that horrifying web of family rituals.

During that homey epilogue to her wedding anniversary, a new phase of her life began. She could only say that at some moment during the family fiesta she broke a crab leg with her hands, and that the dry sound produced by the act left her dazed, that the noise coincided with the popping of the champagne cork, and that a voice seemed to say to her: "They're shooting at the house," as she contemplated, with a disgust that was born in the deepest parts of her being, the mambo steps executed by a quartet of slightly inebriated women, and heard, coming from another part of the room, the reverberating laughter of the male wing, which surely exploded every time Nicolás finished telling an obscene story. She was bewildered by the split personality that could manifest itself in her husband; he could be a dandy in the elegant world into which he'd insinuated himself, and soon after, a rake among the rabble. She also noticed the proper distance her cousin maintained, his restraint, the barrier he established with his icy smile. She knew that the moment she broke a crab leg and heard the popping of a champagne cork, one phase of her life was coming to an end and another, fuller, freer, in which that young man, her cousin, her lover, wouldn't have to listen to anyone's off-color stories, or obey orders, or allow himself to be trampled by the arrogance that Nicolás was capable of employing with his subordinates.

The vision she had was blinding and overpowering. She realized that she wasn't prepared to face it. She began to tremble; she then burst out laughing. She felt as if she were about to cry with joy. She wanted to proclaim her happiness at the top of her voice, shout it with all the force her lungs would allow. But she didn't want to play the part of a hysterical woman before that loathsome band of boors. She would learn to pretend, to hide her emotions until she was free once and for all. She was fed up with having nervous disorders attributed to her since childhood, when in her opinion the scenes that gave rise to such legends were nothing more than manifestations of a more refined sensitivity than that of her sisters. She made up her mind to go to the bathroom, splash water on her face, and inhale a bit of lavender. But as soon as she stood up, despite her firm resolve to resist, to arrive undefeated at the final goal, she felt sobs escape from her breast, which coincided with the noisy popping of another cork. She observed some confusion around her. Inside the sudden wave of irrationality that was about to wash over her, Jacqueline was lucid enough to know that she was on the brink of destroying her victory before she even lifted a finger to achieve it. She'd always prided herself on the speed of her reactions, and that afternoon was no exception. Amid moaning, trembling, and sobbing, she began to scream:

"The ground is shaking! It's shaking! My God, can't everyone tell it's shaking?!"

The astonishment was universal. Everyone tried to find signs of an earthquake. Was anything moving in the house? The lamps? The paintings? The curtains? Nothing! Everything was in its place.

"A well-staged scene to throw us out of the house, I must admit!" exclaimed María Dorotea with an expression of indignation. "Typical María Magdalena! I know her like the back of my hand! I've had to deal with her for many years, but today we won't let her get away with it."

The guests stayed to dance and drink well into the night. With the help of her husband and Alicia Villalba, who was arriving at that moment, Jacqueline was taken to her room and laid on the bed. She cried unconsolably, then gradually calmed down. She looked at herself in the mirror and found herself so horrible that she cried another long while. She got up several times ready to scream for the moochers to get out of her house, to insult them because of the loud music, the clamor caused by their voices and their laughter, but as soon as she stood up, she threw herself back on the bed to continue crying. Every time she looked at herself in the mirror, she suffered a new shock. Her face had become swollen; her half-closed, rat-like eyes provided a glimpse of her pitiful face. The sobs were unable to free her from the oppression she'd experienced during the seven years of marriage she had the misfortune of celebrating that day. With difficulty, with unimaginable difficulty, she managed to get up; she left her room, walked to the staircase, and from there, lying on the floor, next to the handrail, invisible to others, trembling, she began to watch the guests. A wave of wanton drunkenness seemed to have swept over the insolent rabble. She was dismayed to see Gaspar, in shirt sleeves and without a tie, dancing the mambo with open abandon with María Dorotea, who opened her mouth over and over, sticking her tongue in and out, pretending to chew gum, like the most vulgar of showgirls, approaching her cousin, with obscene little steps, thrusting her pelvis into his, then crouching down in front of him with animal-like movements, as if begging for mercy and at the same time seeking copulation, which wasn't merely devoid of any charm but also repugnant. An appalling spectacle! Nothing would have pleased her more than to see Gaspar, collapsed in an armchair, away from the others, his face contorted by misfortune, aware—who knows how!—of the shocking revelation experienced by the woman he loved. She returned, slowly, clinging to the wall, to the master bedroom; the crisis had passed, leaving her in a wake of exaltation and melancholy. Was there any point in running the risks that the immediate future held for her for a man who, during the moments she was overcome by emotion, took pleasure in dancing in the most vulgar way with a woman as cheap as María Dorotea? Her mind suddenly broke into an unbridled gallop. She conceived projects, discarded them; the details of the plan she should follow during the days to come emerged in dizzying series of sparks, intermingling, canceling each other out. The solution seemed within her grasp. Without a doubt, she kept repeating to herself, it was necessary for Gaspar to move forward with the divorce proceedings. The woman he'd married was reluctant to let him go. Jacqueline felt quite confused. The last ten months were the happiest of her life. When Gaspar told her about his marital misfortunes, his concern for the future of his daughters, he caused her to share in his sadness, his fears, transforming her not only into a lover, but also a sister, a friend, and a mother.

She sat down again in front of the mirror, wiped her tears, slathered her face with cold cream. She wiped it with a towel. She studied herself carefully in the mirror and, apparently satisfied, stretched out on the bed, and began to remember.

"The beginning of every love affair in some way resembles the dawn," Márgara Armengol used to say. One morning she stood in front of the mirror and began to get dressed in her most elegant clothes, only to decide a while later to trade them for a skirt and sweater, throw on a raincoat, and add, tilted to one side, an old blue cap. In the middle of her breasts, over her sweater, she placed a small bouquet of costume jewelry daisies; embedded in the center of one of them there was a tiny watch, a brooch her husband made the most distasteful jokes about every time he saw it. As she drove to the Asunción, she felt like a French student who was going on a romantic date for the first time. At the hotel's reception desk she asked the manager, a coarse, unshaven man whose jacket collar was drowning in dandruff, if he knew where she could buy two chains: a thin gold one for her watch that would allow her to suspend it about thirty centimeters from her chest so she wouldn't have to take it off every time she wanted to check the time, and a thick leather one for her dog; That was it, a small gold chain for her and a collar with a leash for her dog, she repeated to the sour-faced fellow, who grudgingly suggested she go to the nearest Sanborn's, the one on Paseo de la Reforma. At that moment Gaspar Rivero appeared, obviously confused by her presence. Jacqueline had no doubt that the intensity of the glances they'd exchanged behind her husband's back on the occasions they'd seen each other at home must have suggested to her cousin that the day was approaching when they'd to meet alone. He politely escorted her to the door of the hotel, where he told her in a low voice that it wasn't advisable to drop by to say hello because Morales, the manager, might know who she was, misinterpret those encounters, and misrepresent them to her husband.

Jacqueline asked at what time it would be wise to come to the hotel without the fear of running into the manager.

"Morales is a dog; I don't know anyone who's a bigger dog than Morales," Gaspar replied. "He spends the whole day at the hotel. If he could, he'd make it his kennel, and he'd never leave so he wouldn't have to spend money on rent or food. He leaves, reluctantly, every Saturday after lunch and doesn't show up again until early Monday morning," Gaspar explained.

And on Friday afternoon that same week Jacqueline phoned him. She said, as was customary, that Nicolás had gone to Cuernavaca; she was sure that he'd gone with one of his frowsy mistresses, but that she wasn't calling to inform him of the details of her married life—there was nothing interesting about that subject—but to ask to meet him the following evening; she'd like for him to know her real world, the one in which she moved like a fish in water. He'd only seen her trapped in hostile milieus, that of Nicolás's employees, or even worse, that of her own relatives, from whom so many things separated her, as he undoubtedly must have noticed by now. What could she possibly have in common, for example, with her brother-in-law Jesús, the foundry worker? Could he tell her? Had he noticed how unpresentable María Dorotea was with that gold crown she had molded in her mouth? The mere act of exchanging greetings with them frayed her nerves. Which is why she wanted them to meet among her true family, not the one that fate had foisted on her but the one she'd chosen voluntarily, a small group of friends who, she was certain, he was going to love. And this was how she came to take him to one of Márgara Armengol's parties. That Saturday she was meticulous in her purchases and in the afternoon dropped off at her friend's house containers of shellfish and asparagus, sausages, hams, various kinds of cheese, nuts, fruit, a wide assortment of beverages. When they arrived at Márgara's house, the guests were listening to an old Elvira Ríos record. Gaspar insisted that they dance; she told him in a quiet voice that it was music for listening, and that, in fact, they weren't in the habit of dancing at her friend's house. She still remembered his spiteful expression; he mumbled something that Jacqueline didn't understand, but which made her decide to dance with him before the mocking gaze of the others. They sat down after two songs. Was it possible that this tense, backward, aloof man was the same cousin whose affable spontaneity she'd found so attractive? It was impossible not to notice that he felt uncomfortable in the midst of the people he described as pretentious, moth-eaten snobs. For the first time it occurred to Jacqueline that these parties could be viewed in a different light from what she was accustomed to. They left early, before midnight, and against her cousin's wishes, she insisted on taking him to the hotel. Jacqueline tried to carry on a conversation; he, on the other hand, answered her in reluctant monosyllables. When they arrived at their destination, she got out of the car and, as if it had been arranged, entered the hotel with Gaspar in the most nonchalant manner possible.

Gaspar Rivero appeared little disposed to invite her to his room; he argued that someone might see them, that the visit would eventually become known, that nothing good could come of such stories; she began to sing under her breath one of Elvira Ríos's songs they'd heard that night: "Darling, I've come back to talk to you again / the night's silence invites me to talk to you . . ." apparently determined not to listen to any argument that might dissuade her. So he had no choice but to let her come in. Jacqueline sat down on the bed and began to undress with all the calmness in the world. On a dresser, she saw a photo in a silver frame of a woman with two little girls beside her. His daughters, he explained. They made love, and she was left with the feeling that the act had lacked something, almost everything, and not because of any physical rather a psychological inadequacy; it seemed to her that her cousin had possessed her out of a sense of duty, by remote control, through an intermediary, which instead of discouraging her left her wanting to return to the charge until he was able to overcome a reluctance driven by fear. The pungent smell that permeated his body aroused her more than any of his caresses. They smoked a duo of cigarettes while still in bed. Jacqueline compared her cousin's lean, gnarled brown body to her own round, white one. For a moment she felt ashamed and covered herself with the sheets; then she remembered that on one occasion or another she'd heard it said that skinny men had a special predilection for corpulence, that is, for chubby women, and she smiled. When Gaspar went into the bathroom to take a shower, Jacqueline took advantage of the opportunity to inspect the room a bit and to search his pockets. She was astonished by the thick wad of bills in his wallet. A fortune! Her surprise was even greater when she discovered in his wallet the oval photo of a woman different than that with the girls on the dresser. She got dressed quickly. She felt as if she were on the verge of exploding with resentment. As he came out of the bathroom, she fired without warning a barrage of indignant questions at him. Why had he told her he was about to get a divorce when he had his wife's photo in view to enjoy when he went to bed and when he woke up? And the other one? Which one? Had he forgotten, perhaps, about the broad whose picture he kept in his pocket? Did he believe, perhaps, that he didn't know that he was carrying the photo of that bimbo, that bona fide whore, in the pocket over his heart? She stood up, mustering what little dignity she had left, ready to leave immediately.

"Don't try to see me again. I'd rather eat snake meat than come back to this dump," she told him, putting the oval photograph in her handbag, and sniffing loudly as if the room gave off a repulsive stench. Her mouth was bitter, her gaze lost. He was combing his hair with obvious composure in front of a mirror, not paying much attention to her. He settled for telling her that he'd never have imagined that she'd stoop so low as to go rummaging through his clothes; he asked her to return the photograph, she let out a shrill laugh and said in a loud voice that he could take it from her by force if he was man enough, that she wouldn't be intimidated by the threat of scandal. She would scream like a madwoman, and her husband could find out what was going on if it came to that; she'd tell him then that his little model employee—the one who pretended to be a meek, honest young man from the provinces—was carrying a fortune in his wallet, and see how he could explain that little fact. Gaspar knotted his tie, put on his jacket, showed her the door, and escorted her to the car without saying a word. When she arrived home, Jacqueline stuck four pins in the photo: two in the eyes, one in the mouth, and another in the middle of the forehead.

A month or so later, she had the idea to organize another one of those little get-togethers she despised so much. The pungent smell of her cousin's body had become an obsession. It wasn't the typical stench of bad hygiene, but an internal odor, perhaps the result of some endocrinal function. The gathering didn't amuse her in the slightest, but it seemed indispensable under the circumstances. She asked her husband to invite Gaspar, but he forgot to do so, and the family party was a disaster. She knew that some people considered her broadmindedness a sign of vulgarity; she invited people who claimed that by merely observing María Dorotea, María del Carmen, and their husbands for five minutes it was possible to know exactly what true commonness was. On that occasion she started off bored to death and then, when she was convinced that her cousin wasn't coming, she began to seethe more and more. Finally, she began to tell a few home truths to those present, who reciprocated in kind. When addressing her, they called her María Magdalena, which drove her to distraction. The words they exchanged on that occasion were so unpleasant that the family get-togethers at the Lobatos' home ended forever.

And one fine day Nicolás showed up accompanied by Gaspar Rivero at lunchtime. Over coffee the cousins began to exchange a few words; it was then that the relationship's true golden age began. Jacqueline had lost weight; she acquired a new, more reserved, wardrobe. She stopped attending the parties at Márgara Armengol's home; she visited her friend only very occasionally to share passionate confidences, to which her confidant responded, reminding her that her home was always open to both of them. Immediately, despite his characteristic shyness, she'd noticed the quality of that young man, asking her in passing for her help organizing a cocktail party that she was thinking of throwing for a young writer on the publication of his last book, for a playwright on his upcoming nuptials, or for a painter on a recent exhibition, adding that of course she was relying on her presence on those occasions. As for her cousin, it went without saying, she considered him a permanent guest.

Fine. Now, for this story to make sense, we need to return to the moment marked by the cracking sound of the crab leg and the firing of the champagne cork. The moment that determined the fate of our dear Jacqueline! During that night and the days that followed, she reviewed the sum of grievances that made up her married life. She was determined to act, but she had to be very cautious in the way she dealt with her cousin. Gaspar was too sensitive, she told herself; he lacked her strength. He wouldn't understand her need for revenge after so many years of her husband's affronts. He was a good boy, innocent. She began, then, by telling him how much she suffered at the thought of him, of both of them, of the suffocating love they were living, with a meager present, without any future. She saw no solution. If she got a divorce, Nicolás could leave her penniless and her cousin unemployed. Live a life of want again? Not on your life! It was unbearable, she said, that her husband could put his hands on her, that he could take control of her body whenever he wanted. No one could imagine how brutal, how abusive he could be in such circumstances. For several days she did nothing but repeat that speech, referring to the immense fortune Lobato had acquired, a man unworthy of enjoying such comfort, a cretin bent on squandering his wealth on second-rate hookers, and then she insisted again that the money should belong to him, to Gaspar, who, at twenty-six, in the prime of his talents, was really the one who deserved it. "If he had Nicolás's money, life would be a paradise!" she said, lying on one of the rickety beds of the Hotel Asunción. Or would it? Did he dare to contradict her? She imagined fantastic scenes, which inevitably culminated in a gondola ride through the canals of Venice. At first, the laughter with which Gaspar received these comments betrayed a hint of apprehension, as if the mere fact of hearing a daring joke might compromise him; then he gradually succumbed to his mistress's constant sermonizing, as Jacqueline no longer knew how to talk about any other subject. And so they began—he, in the same cautious way he'd listened to her at the start, as if it were only a game, and she, now unfettered—to plan one by one the necessary steps, until the fantasy vanished altogether, and they found themselves talking with absolute candor. Jacqueline offered vital details: in the house there was a pistol. Nicolás kept it at the bottom of the center drawer of his desk, and the sooner she showed it to him, the better. From a certain moment on, they must stop seeing each other to avoid suspicion, and they would meet only when Nicolás invited him to the house to eat. Gaspar said he'd accompany Nicolás some weekends; he had asked him to do so several times, he wanted to involve him in the work he was doing in Cuernavaca. They would behave with absolute naturalness, they would act with the utmost discretion, they would live apart until the time came to make the despicable tyrant kiss the dust. Jacqueline felt a delicious shudder run through her as she listened to that expression. The only condition she made was that she not be the one to shoot. In the first place, she'd never held a pistol in her hands; in the second, it was a task that didn't correspond to a spouse. She, for example, wouldn't dare ask Gaspar to murder his wife. There were things that could be done and others that couldn't: they were out of the question.

Before the agreed-upon separation, they analyzed all the details of the project to eliminate Nicolás Lobato. On one occasion, Gaspar arrived very agitated. He spoke nonstop, which at times made what he was saying almost unintelligible. He'd just visited one of the three most prominent lawyers in Mexico City, he recounted, who'd promised to handle his divorce in a few weeks. The attorney would begin by investigating his wife. He had the best agents, so if Rosario was whoring around, they'd find out in short order with whom and where she was doing it, which meant she was screwed. If they found out she wasn't involved with anyone—which he doubted, since he knew her appetite very well—they'd be able arrange a chance encounter with a gigolo. There were some very skilled ones, types who never fail. One fine day they'd find the door to the henhouse open and the rooster inside. Immediately the cameras would go to work; with flash, with anything necessary. They'd catch the boyfriend with his hands in the cookie jar, as they say. From that moment, he'd be in a position to demand, like it or not, that she consent to the divorce. Money was needed. Starting that day Gaspar began to ask her for what seemed to her like exorbitant sums, but which, despite the repulsion she felt at the methods described by her cousin to defeat his wife and the language he used to refer to her, she handed over without hesitation. On one occasion, she was obliged to give him the pearl necklace that Nicolás had once given her in Rome so he could pawn it.

From the first night she'd slept with Gaspar, she'd felt an overriding need to make love to her husband. As the plans to assassinate him progressed, her passion increased proportionately. Nicolás Lobato was frankly surprised by the pleasure he received on these occasions, which no woman had ever equaled. In Jacqueline, the two men created, by complementing each other, a new erotic entity: Gaspar's reluctance was enhanced by Nicolás's aggressiveness. The smell of her husband's soap and deodorant coupled with her cousin's arousing stench.

They had to be precise, they repeated: nail down a series of details, leave no loose ends. Gaspar believed the elimination of Nicolás Lobato should take place on the road to Cuernavaca. That day she'd express her desire to accompany him to see the construction underway in Las Palmas; she'd say that she'd then go on to Tepoztlán, where she'd meet some of her old classmates from university for lunch. She would leave with Nicolás. They would convince him to travel, under the pretext of showing him an old house under demolition whose doors, beams, and ironwork were going to be put up for sale, to a ranch accessible through the old highway, which would allow them to avoid any checkpoint where someone might identify them. Gaspar would drive Jacqueline's car in whose glove compartment he'd find the pistol. The Lobatos would stop at an often-deserted spot on the highway, where Gaspar would be waiting to guide them down a dirt road. When they got out of the car, the lover would approach Nicolás from behind and shoot him at point-blank range, so as not to miss. Then he and Jacqueline would return to the capital in her car. Each one would prepare their alibi. It wouldn't be difficult. She would call Márgara. As soon as the conversation began, she'd tell her friend to excuse her for a moment, that someone was knocking at the door and ask her to please call her back in five minutes. That way she could prove that she was at home in Mexico City that afternoon. Gaspar would walk into the hotel restaurant repeatedly to be seen by the employees and customers; then he'd lock himself in his room and order a beer and some snacks over the phone. Something like that. The notion that each of them had spent the afternoon in the city would become fixed in the mind of various people. No personal documents would be left on Nicolás's body or inside the car. It would take time for the police to identify the corpse. Perhaps more than a day would pass without them contacting her to inform her that her husband had been murdered. A number of details remained to be worked out. Inventing, for example, explanations in the event they were unlucky enough to be seen by an acquaintance returning together, which, although unlikely, had to be considered. She had to talk to the maid and ask that she change her day off from Sunday to Saturday, so that on the specified date there would be no witnesses to the goings-on in the house.

And so the project evolved. Gaspar Rivero began to study the highway and its possibilities. They stopped being seen together. They agreed to telephone each other only if necessary and to speak in code. In case of emergency, they would meet at a prearranged spot: the Zaplana Bookstore on Avenida Juárez, where, hidden behind the bookshelves, they could talk safely. They set the date for the crime. Jacqueline felt safe, very close to eliminating the obstacle that stood between her and her happiness.

One night, shortly before the appointed day, Nicolás Lobato came home accompanied by Gaspar. They had dinner and then, when the two men went into the living room to play a game of dominoes, began to talk in low voices about something inaccessible to her, a mystery. Jacqueline couldn't resist the temptation to see the liberating weapon, to hold it in her hands, to caress it. She considered the impulse morbid, but she couldn't resist. Opening the desk drawer, where the revolver lay, she saw an envelope of photographs and, out of mere inertia—out of no real curiosity, she could swear—she opened it. In it were several color photos of three couples in bathing suits. She recognized Nicolás with a young girl, undoubtedly one of his employees, and Gaspar, kissing a woman who was baring her breasts. She didn't know why, but at that moment she was sure it was the same tramp whose photo she'd stuck the pins in. Yes, there was no doubt in her mind that it was the same floozy whose face she encountered in Gaspar's wallet the first night they were together. It's not clear how she managed to not go mad forever at that instant. Her cousin, with that damn angelic face, had for months played her for a fool. He had taken money from her hand over fist. With a clairvoyance that astonished her, she glimpsed her future: after Nicolás Lobato's funeral, Gaspar would pretend to love her even more; in due time he'd marry her, and then, at the first opportunity, he'd send her to the next life, just as he intended to do with her poor husband, to inherit a tidy fortune that he'd lay at the feet of the naked whore he was kissing in the photos. With a skittish movement she seized the pistol. A terrifying scream, followed by another and another, escaped her throat. She tried to head for the living room, but in her confusion, she went out a different door and suddenly found herself in the garden, in the dark. She fired the first shot into the air. She was screaming, howling, her face awash with tears, wanting to die, but to first take pleasure in killing her traitorous lover. She'd fallen into his clutches like an imbecile! The men ran to stop her. She fired two, three, four more times, without knowing at what or at whom. She felt a blow to her face, something slimy and salty melted in her mouth. She felt another blow and then her head being wrapped in a heavy cloth. She realized she was being beaten and that her hand holding the revolver twisted. A surprising heat ran through her right arm from her shoulder to her fingertips. The rest was chaos. She remembers a sting, an injection in her arm by a stranger. Sometime later, she awoke in a white room that at first she was unable to identify; a woman sitting by her bedside was asking her to calm down: a nurse. The only thing she understood was that she didn't want to live; for the next few days she refused to accept any food, she was kept on an IV, whenever a doctor or nurse came in, she refused to utter a word, and did nothing but cry. On numerous occasions she saw her mother sitting in front of her; she heard her mother defending her husband, telling her that Nicolás was suffering, that he was very tormented, that the only thing he wanted was to see her recover, and later he was there too, at her side, kissing her hand, her cheeks, but she didn't really understand what he was saying to her, and there were times when her room was full of people: her mother, her husband, her two sisters, a nurse scolding her in a contrived childlike voice, waving an admonishing finger at her, as is customary with little girls when they engage in mischief. Little by little she made concessions to the world, her desire to die diminished; one day she tasted food, they removed the IV, and she began to talk to the doctors, to the nurses, even to Nicolás. Then the day arrived when her husband showed up with a suitcase. From it, the nurse took out the dress she'd worn for the first time the day of their wedding anniversary and helped her get dressed. Nicolás draped a fur coat over her shoulders and placed on her finger a ring with a beautiful emerald. She burst into tears, rested her head on her husband's chest, and, like this, locked in an embrace, treated with a tenderness she could never have imagined from such a barbarian, they left the room, reached the car, and once again found themselves at home. As Nicolás placed her on her bed she began to weep silently again. She told herself that she accepted the coat and ring so not to cause an unnecessary scandal at the hospital, but that she'd never wear them again. She had no desire or energy to speak. She had no interest in asking any questions. In some way it was nice to feel the warmth and strength that emanated from her husband's body. Nicolás, since they entered the bedroom, didn't speak either; he stretched her out on the bed, caressed her hands, and then, his voice choking, told her that she'd been a fool, a little fool, an immense fool, that she was the only woman who meant anything to him, that he couldn't understand how she could doubt that, and that now she had to be good and sleep, and they would both forget sooner than they could imagine the silliness of the past, that he needed her, that he loved her, that he loved her, that he loved her . . .

CHAPTER 3

SHE LIVED WITH HER SADNESS in tow. She'd come out of one crisis only to sink into another. At times her migraines were so debilitating she could barely move her head. Neck and back pains left her paralyzed for several days. She consulted numerous doctors, including a few psychiatrists; she talked to them about everything: her childhood traumas, Nicolás's infidelities, which more than once, she told them, and she almost believed it, had led her to the brink of suicide; her thirst to know: the antidote to all her misfortunes. A sort of parrot unable to interrupt the endless stream of lamentations. But at all times she kept an iron silence about her love affair with Gaspar Rivero and the criminal plot hatched by her and her cousin. She didn't know if she was really getting help from the doctors: they would prescribe her pills that dried out her mouth and caused her to act like an automaton, if not fall asleep at all hours. As soon as she was convinced that the treatment wasn't working, she changed doctors. She thought she'd never get over the shame of having been outwitted in such a despicable way by that rogue who, while bewitching her with his acidic body odor, swore his eternal love. She could never have suspected the magnitude of her naïveté, her stupidity, her inability to notice a link in the chain of deceit in which she'd been a victim; after the crisis, the mirror woven with lies became so clear to her, so evident, that only a blind person could have failed to see it. Every time Nicolás Lobato came to see her, he usually found her lying on the bed drowning in an air of desolation. She always had a book open beside her, which she seemed unable to focus on reading. If he asked her how she was feeling, she'd invariably cry, get out of bed dejectedly, walk clumsily, lay her head on her husband's chest, embrace him, and continue to sob even more forlornly.

One afternoon, Nicolás commented that he'd decided to leave Coyoacán. It was necessary to forget the recent events. He was about to buy a home in Polanco, on Calle Julio Verne, where they would start a new life. A large house, unfortunately in poor condition, with just-the-right-size garden. One of the architects working on Las Palmas would begin to restore it as soon as he had some free time. Life still had extraordinary moments in store for them, she'd soon see. Incidentally, he wanted the deeds to the house to be in her name; in a few days he'd impose on her to accompany him to the notary to sign the necessary documents.

Jacqueline never asked again about Gaspar Rivero, who gradually disappeared from her life. There were weeks when she barely remembered him; when she did, it was with genuine hatred. One day she received a wholly unpleasant visit from María Dorotea, who for more than half and an hour did nothing but repeat a string of banalities, and then, as if it were impossible for her to contain herself, let slip that Gaspar was living in Cuernavaca, where he was supervising the work at Las Palmas. She commented that the previous week she'd gone there with Jesús, her husband, who'd been entrusted with the ironwork. She described with exasperating laggardness the state of the work. She said that in a small already-completed section, on a table, a model of the entire complex was on display. Absolutely magnificent, she exclaimed, wide-eyed, yes, something never-before seen, a dream, a large tract of land far, though not too far, from the city, a bouquet of wonders. In the center stood the grand hotel, surrounded by a garden that had the makings of being something fantastic. In the middle of a forest of palms, the tennis courts, the stables, the swimming pools. On one side of the parcel, they were building a row of bungalows and on the opposite side, an apartment building with hotel service. The model included everything, even the golf course and other sports facilities. Seeing it with her own eyes, she repeated, licking her lips with excessive vulgarity, she realized that this was a monumental enterprise, a dream of a thousand and one nights, a legend. And she repeated time and time again that Nicolás was a businessman of great stature, with more business savvy than anyone could imagine. A gentleman and a mogul! Nothing displeased Jacqueline so much than seeing her sister gesticulate with the same decidedly common theatricality that she'd seen since her early school years. From her sister she learned several things she didn't know; for example, that Nicolás had sold the Hotel Asunción, to meet the tremendous costs that the construction was incurring. Las Palmas would end up eating Nicolás's shirt, if he wasn't careful, the know-it-all continued. In the years to come, even after the hotel opened, the construction would devour not only the other hotel but perhaps even the travel agency, but the time would come when the problems would disappear. Nicolás would obtain a mortgage loan, and, if necessary, he could sell shares in the bungalows and apartments with hotel service. Nicolás Lobato would show the world what he was capable of.

She'd never, for as long as she could remember, gotten along with her sisters, and, as time went by, María Dorotea—by far the worst!—had become unbearable. She loathed them, among other reasons, for refusing to respect her wishes. She'd never succeeded in getting them to call her Jacqueline; they remained invested in her old name, which she abhorred—María Magdalena—pronouncing it with a mocking singsong that drove her to distraction. Since they were children, both of them had adopted the same competitive attitude towards her, the youngest, which grew stronger to the point of souring any vestige of a friendly relationship. Dealing with them, indulging their husbands during the period when Gaspar Rivero was taking advantage of her, on more than one occasion seemed beyond her strength. She'd done it to create a semblance of normalcy to her cousin's presence at home. It was now necessary to make them understand that this period was part of an unrepeatable past. Jacqueline received the information that Gaspar continued to work at her husband's side with a sangfroid that she herself described as admirable and which confounded her sister entirely; not a single facial muscle moved at the mention of that detestable name. María Dorotea was unable to perceive even a wisp of the flash of rage that gripped her sister at the mention of that son of a bitch who'd almost destroyed her marriage. And she took pleasure in not offering the slightest comment on the great work that this painfully boring woman, turned spokesperson for Las Palmas, described in a voice that varied without rhyme or reason from schmaltzy to shrill. Upon observing Jacqueline's indifference in the conversation, María Dorotea dove headfirst into the only subject that on that occasion really interested her:

"Yes, yes, yes...what terrific luck for Nicolás that this cousin of ours has settled there," syntax had never been her forte. "Gaspar will be loyal; he'll forget the problems of the past. A noble, healthy, faithful boy. More than once I've recommended to him: 'Take a sponge to your memory, my boy, and act as if you just met her husband.' You'll see, María Magdalena, he'll end up forgetting the bad times you put him through, your hopeless efforts to trap him. He owes Nicolás so much that he'll repay him with loyalty. I don't want to pry in other people's affairs; everyone is the master of their own destiny. Nicolás is a naïve man, he's good, he loves you, but all blindness has its limits..."

"Evil comes from ignorance," she said, mimicking the tone of María Dorotea's voice. "It's the fruit of bad taste, of vulgarity. You don't know how much it would please me to share with you the talks I participate in on Saturday nights at Márgara Armengol's home. How I'd love for us to begin to talk...we couldn't do it when we were younger, our cursed poverty robbed us of that opportunity...about *The Brothers Karamazov*, *The Metamorphosis*, or *Les Demoiselles d'Avignon* by the famous Picasso! I'd love to give you and María del Carmen those opportunities that life has denied both of you. But what can I do?! Here I am, talking like a street vendor, when this afternoon I've an appointment with my doctor, an admirable man, I assure you; he insists that I start writing. According to him, I should start with a short story; don't misunderstand me, I'm more than willing to describe the frustration of mediocre people, their resentment towards everything that is superior to them, towards what they'll never be able to achieve. I'd have to set my story in an imaginary city, and in a different era from ours, so as not to run the risk of someone recognizing herself, don't you think? And here I am, still talking! I'm going, I'm going!"

She stood up, and without so much as holding out her hand to her sister she bid her good afternoon, picked up a magazine from a table and went into her room.

She knew María Dorotea well; she imagined the heavy rain of anonymous letters that would soon descend on her house. She had to act immediately, to take the necessary precautions. In the aftermath of that conversation with her sister, the abulia that had afflicted her in the previous months disappeared. That day, Nicolás didn't come home for lunch or dinner; she waited for him until late that night and finally fell asleep without seeing him. Since the great crisis, they'd slept in separate rooms, so she was unable to follow his movements closely. The next day, she had breakfast alone, dressed even more smartly than usual, and, without warning, went to the travel agency.

Nicolás was shocked to see her enter his office. Before he could open his mouth, Jacqueline stole the floor. She spoke in a neutral voice, vigorous and distant, like a television broadcaster at news time:

"Are you surprised by my visit? Yesterday, my sister María Dorotea came to see me. Do you know what a hyena like her is capable of? She revealed to me, without omitting any detail, your new infidelities." To her own surprise, as she uttered that lie, her face grew flush, her voice trembled, her eyes clouded with tears that were on the verge of flowing. "I am and have been a woman who respects herself." She felt that she'd lost her course. "Correct me if I'm lying. I've led an abominable life at your side...I'm a woman who's convalescing . . . Above all, I'm concerned with my spiritual improvement . . . I've not given you the happiness you desired...you've sought it on your own . . ." Tears were streaming down her cheeks. She realized that it was necessary to get to the point, before Nicolás emerged from his stupor. Amid her tears, she raised her voice, achieving a frightening and pathetic effect. "I've been insulted! Slandered! María Dorotea told me, with her characteristic sordidness, that that miserable accomplice you keep in Cuernavaca, unfortunately my relative, assured her that I was chasing him, you can imagine to what end..." The whining disappeared from her voice and was replaced with a fit of rage. "My life is transparent, and you can't tolerate that! You'd rather I were a stupid little whore, that I were equal to you in vices, in lust! That would justify your treating me the way you do. I've come to tell you that I'm leaving your house. I'm leaving the way I came. I could have left with my suitcases so that when you got home there'd be no sign of me. I preferred to show my face. You'll soon know my address. If you want a divorce, you'll have it. If you want me to come back, I'll do that too. But for that to happen, and I imagine it won't be at all easy, you'll have to get rid of your accomplice, banish him from us for good; I imagine he's got you by the short hairs, he must know something that you not even dared to confide in me; I can't explain the relationship between the two of you in any other way." She picked up her gloves, her black bag, and made an exit to great effect, like those she'd seen certain actresses make at a movie's climax.

Nicolás Lobato rose calmly from his seat, raced to the door, opened it, went out with Jacqueline and drove her in his car to a restaurant, insisting that it would be more pleasant to converse there than in his office. From the conversation that followed, it was made known that on the following Saturday he'd fire Gaspar, and that in a couple of months they would leave for Europe, where they'd been only once before, shortly after they were married, twelve or thirteen years before.

Everything happened just that way: Gaspar left Las Palmas and they spent five weeks in Europe. For the rest of her life Jacqueline never saw or heard from her cousin again. At times, many years later, she remembered the pungent smell of his body, which would leave her troubled for a long while.

Shortly after returning from Europe, Jacqueline received a visit from Márgara Armengol. It had been almost a year since they'd seen each other. In the last months of her relationship with Gaspar Rivero, she stopped seeing her. Jacqueline was offended because, after her illness, she'd called her friend, who refused to visit her or answer her calls. Upon seeing her, she forgot her resentment and began to share some of her impressions of Europe. It would have been ideal that they take a trip together, she said; the energy of one and the culture of the other would have made for the perfect experience. Márgara seemed much more serious, almost solemn, her sense of humor obviously diminished. She replied that friends continued to meet at her home, but less frequently. The times were different, the tone of the get-togethers had changed, more elevated, one could say. Their salad days were behind them. Each age, she added censoriously, had different needs and requirements. She'd decided to transform her home in Coyoacán into an Academy.

"People, in general," she explained, "have an undeveloped talent and are eager to know and at the same time make their voices heard, but they don't know how to do it. In our small Academy, a group of friends are committed to providing the necessary elements to people with certain concerns and thus enable them to take a leap that until now seemed impossible to them. Think about your case, Jacqueline. For someone like you, who left university halfway through, but who is bubbling over with intellectual curiosity, our courses won't only enable you to broaden your knowledge, but also to reveal some unexpressed creative abilities." She explained that there would be a workshop on literary creation (where students would learn the essentials for writing short stories and novels), a course on the great storytellers (to be titled "Hermeneutics of the Novel," in which both classic and contemporary novelists would be studied), and another one on the history of the visual arts. Classes would be given in the morning. She would be in charge of the hermeneutics course; Julián Barreda would lead the workshop on literary creation, and a young man of Italian extraction, Gianni Ferraris, intelligent, a discovery, a real delight, would cultivate his audience on the high points of art history, from Altamira to the present. "Ferraris won't only talk about painting and sculpture," she added, "as the teachers of this specialty routinely do, but he'll also be in charge of other visual media, photography, film, for example. In short, we'll introduce any innovation we deem appropriate. Professor Marina Villalobos, that apostle of Mexico's past, will organize excursions to sites of historical or artistic interest. We want to have a flexible program, eliminating the rigidness and pedantry that do nothing but scare students away. And so you can judge for yourself and then give me your opinion, because I'm sure that you'll not pass up the chance to enroll in my little temple of knowledge."

Jacqueline enrolled immediately in the narrative workshop and in the course on the hermeneutics of the novel. The results weren't long in coming: she began to write some stories about her unhappy childhood, enriched her library with a good number of novels and a treatise on contemporary literature. Every Tuesday and Thursday she attended classes at Márgara's home with a sort of vague mystical elan. It was a happy and peaceful period, but unfortunately very brief. She read, meditated, wrote, discussed. She managed to express herself with relative fluency both orally and in writing. She tried on some occasions to share her experiences with her husband, but Nicolás responded with the same indifference he'd have shown had she attended a ladies' get-together for crochet or cross-stitch and then persisted in explaining the methods she'd learned that day. The courses were, from many points of view, a success. The social life at Márgara Armengol's house changed remarkably. The conversation turned academic. She'd never read so much in her life! Gianni Ferraris, the professor of Italian extraction, came across as a foul-smelling pain in the neck during their first casual exchanges, but after some hesitation she ended up enrolling in his course, and from the first class she found his teaching exceptional. Shortly thereafter she also enrolled in Marina Villalobos's Mexican Art course, and in doing so doubled her weekly attendance at the Academy. Enrolling in Marina's course allowed her to participate in the excursions to pre-Hispanic and colonial sites that took place on the first Saturday of each month. At the end of the semester, a long weekend was chosen to undertake more ambitious trips. In early May there would be an excursion to the Yucatán.

She suggested to her husband that they make the trip together. She did so without the slightest enthusiasm; it was a merely formal invitation, as she was sure that Nicolás would not fail to go to Cuernavaca to check on the progress of the construction for any reason. If he did venture to go, his crass comments would take all the pleasure out of the trip. She remembered with dismay the elephant-like sensitivity he'd repeatedly shown during their European tour. During the last days of their stay in Rome, she feigned a constant migraine so that she'd have to go out with him as little as possible. His comments even made her ill. Fortunately, Nicolás declined the invitation; he proposed that she go with Alicia Villalba, but she replied that it was out of the question, that she didn't want to become a source of gossip for the group, that being the case, she preferred to go alone; that wasn't possible either, because on the eve of the trip to Mérida her mother died, and she couldn't and wouldn't back out of her filial obligations. Only in the third year of taking courses, in April 1964, was she finally able to fly to Yucatán. María Villalobos's group consisted of about twenty travelers, including Gianni Ferraris, who, like her, was unacquainted with the peninsula. They flew to Mérida in adjoining seats, and during their first days in Yucatán, except on brief occasions, they were inseparable. She found chatting with him incredibly pleasant, listening as he recounted his family's history, learning about his plans, the most important of which was to settle in Italy in a couple of years and stay there indefinitely. Even more interesting were their walks around Mérida and excursions to Uxmal and Chichén Itzá, hearing his observations about Mayan art and its comparisons with other cultures. Among the notebooks left in Cuernavaca was one that gathered Ferraris's comments on the most diverse cultural, social, and even personal topics. During that trip, Jacqueline fell head over heels for the Mayan ruins, and also in love, when, one afternoon, in the hotel bar, while having a coffee, as she was writing postcards and waiting for the Italian professor, with whom she'd arranged to take a stroll around Mérida and later dine in a restaurant that served local dishes, by pure chance she met David Carranza, a dark and debonair young man, who in many ways was the antithesis of Ferraris, who sat next to her and immediately struck up a conversation, impressing her such that minutes later she snuck off with him, went dancing and, what's more, invited him to spend the night in her bed.

She could barely sleep. In the early morning, as the first rays of light entered the room, she studied the young man's face with rapture, marveling at the sensuality of his perfect mouth; she then gently ran her hand over his hairy chest, his groin, thighs, penis, and began to rub his body with the other one, such that soon after he again caressed, overpowered, and penetrated her, convincing her that the inadequate sexual relationship with her cousin had been a mere preamble to the plenitude of that moment. As the group was about to return to Mexico City, David Carranza invited her to spend a week in Cozumel. Jacqueline telephoned her husband, made up a confusing and incoherent story about the possibility of extending the trip to Cozumel and perhaps Isla Mujeres with some classmates, and then headed for the airport with her new lover.

During the day they took sun and swam, danced at night, made love until dawn, before sinking into an exhausted sleep. She spoke to him in earnest about her courses, about the reason for her visit to Mérida, not wanting to be thought of as a common tourist. David listened to her patiently with a polite smile, and finally explained that culture seemed to him a very respectable proposition, he had to admit, but that his real interests lay in another area of knowledge: politics. He held a position in the Ministry of Labor. He'd been offered a no-show job: it wasn't necessary to show up at the office except for paydays, his political godfather—who recommended him for the position—told him. But he didn't think that attitude was appropriate, considering it, in the short and long term, a threat to his political future. He went to the Ministry every day, managed to talk to his superiors, maintained the best possible relations with his colleagues, especially with Manuel de Gracia, his fellow countryman, with whom he shared the protection of the same godfather and whom he distrusted completely, and attended any breakfast with officials that was available to him.

That was his life. There, in Cozumel, he purchased all the newspapers that arrived from Mexico City, read the political columns attentively, commented on them to her, or rather, explained them to her from beginning to end, while they lounged beside the pool. Talking about the political and administrative life of the country was his greatest delight. He might not have learned anything about law, but his legal studies had allowed him to make the right connections. No sooner had he arrived from his native Campeche than he began to move in university politics. He stressed that a politician of quality should take great pains with his appearance. It was a career that was far from easy. One had to run for an hour as soon as he got out of bed, go to the gym three times a week, choose the right clothes with the utmost care. To remain alert to the excessive ambitions of machinators, like Manuel de Gracia, for example, whose hunger to climb the ladder was so boundless that it could only be compared to his lack of ethical principles. Jacqueline adopted such an expression as she listened to him that anyone would think she was in the presence of a titan. During the pauses he allowed, she'd tell him tidbits of her life, talk about her frustrations and tortures, about the uncouth husband who used to belittle others with one derisive phrase or another, and who, frankly, had no interests. Could he imagine, she asked with guile, someone who detested everything that had to do with public life, to the point of repeating at every turn that every politician in the world, but especially in Mexico, were out-and-out crooks, if not total morons, and that it would be impossible to make a whole man out of all of them put together?

She told him over and over that he was different from any man she'd ever known; she lied to him when she assured him that she was experiencing her first marital infidelity, and she adored discovering in David the same brazenness of language and attitudes that Nicolás Lobato used when he made love to her. Suddenly, his velvety tone when speaking, his elegant gestures, and the cardboard language with which he patiently told her about every step he took to make a place for himself in the political sphere all suddenly disappeared; then the wild beast appeared. And what a beast!

From the first moment she was aware of the exaggerated vanity of her Don Juan. With a modicum of intelligence, she told herself, any woman could have him in her clutches. All that was necessary was to feign constant admiration and interest in his presence. She had the admiration, but no interest in what he was saying. After two or three attempts at conversation, she accepted with resignation that she couldn't demand of him the same appreciation she had for culture. She also noticed that when they engaged in conversation with other couples at the bar or restaurant, he enjoyed listening to her talk about Mayan archaeology, books, or music, as if it were a universe intimately shared by both of them, which filled her with satisfaction and made her forgive his inadequacies in those areas.

When they returned to Mexico City, their relationship continued. Shortly after returning from Cozumel David had been offered, he said, a position at the Mexican Embassy in Rome. He turned it down because he didn't want to be away from his true interests. He didn't want to go into exile. He began to work in public relations for a senator who aspired to the governorship of his state. He was charged, along with a team of colleagues from the most diverse disciplines, with devising a plan of action for him; a difficult task, he said energetically, since it was more than a simple matter of formulating a model rather a real paradigm of government. Someone, the godfather of course, had imposed on the group the presence of the ineffable Manuel de Gracia, who never failed to miss an opportunity to steal the limelight and obscure the work of the others in the process. David never understood what those words meant; the following, however, was clearer to him: the senator in question had promised to obtain for him, once his candidacy was launched, a position as private secretary to the senior officer of the Ministry of the Navy. Then came two or three inexplicable setbacks. Not only did he not obtain the coveted private secretary position, but for unknown reasons, about which the only thing that seemed evident to him was the artful intervention of Manuel de Gracia, he lost the senator's protection, also that of his political godfather, and, consequently, the post at the Ministry of Labor, where he only appeared, as he confessed in a moment of carelessness, on paydays to collect his salary.

One rainy afternoon, in the scant and impersonal apartment occupied by David Carranza in Colonia Condesa, after fornicating freely and pleasurably, Jacqueline, in a state of obvious exaltation, assured him that his misfortunes arose from the fact that he was too noble, that nothing in his person concealed his greatness, which surely aroused the envy and resentment of that foul pack of resentful, frustrated, middling social climbers who surrounded him, which Carranza resignedly acknowledged; he needed, she added, capital to back him so that he could embark on the realization of his dreams on a grand scale, not squander his talents being someone's secretary; to have at his disposal a newspaper, for example, that could help enhance his personality. It wasn't fair that a few miserable people got everything while vilifying those who endeavored to ennoble politics. No, it wasn't fair; no matter how many arguments he offered, he wouldn't be able to convince her. Ever since their meeting—she spoke as if saying a prayer—she'd done nothing but think that, in the event of her husband's death, she, as his sole heir, would have the necessary fortune to help David grow, to help show others what greatness David Carranza was capable of. She repeated the campaign of seduction she'd used with her cousin Gaspar. To her surprise and delight, she didn't have to overcome any resistance. The aspiring politician, after an instant of momentary astonishment, welcomed with all the naturalness in the world the mission of sending Nicolás Lobato to the next life.

"To think that I don't even know your husband!" he exclaimed. "No matter. We've got to plan this affair with the utmost care; in my opinion, contracting a hitman would be the least prudent solution. I don't think there would be a possibility of mutual interests; whatever goon we contacted would end up extorting or blackmailing us, leaving us in the poorhouse, if not the cemetery. This won't be an easy undertaking. We'll have to make do with our own resources, run him over, suffocate him, whatever . . . It seems that it would be in our interest to make it look like someone else, Manuel de Gracia, for example, was the mastermind of the crime. The sooner we act, the better!"

"We'll need a gun," said Jacqueline, as if she were instructing a preschooler. The tone of her voice and mannerisms often took on the qualities of an actress in a didactic play. "The fact that you don't know my husband is in your favor. Moreover, no one knows that I come to visit you. No one either associates you or will associate you with me or Nicolás. I'll sneak you into the house; we'll feign a robbery. Do you know how to shoot? I'll leave my car outside and give you the keys so you can get away easily; then you'll leave the car wherever you want. There'll be no servants that day. I'll guide you, David. Trust me. A great future is awaiting you, and I want to accompany you in all the grand scenarios that destiny has in store for you."

"And how would we implicate that son of a bitch De Gracia?"

The answer was always the same:

"We must forget about that machinator. Any incidental complication could ruin us."

As had happened during her previous love affair, Jacqueline spent her nights in a kind of erotic delirium. She made love at home with such violent fury and desperation that Nicolás Lobato was dumbstruck, convinced that he'd never be able to take all of her in, convinced that no matter what happened she'd always be the woman of his life, the real one, the only one, proving that with each passing year he became more passionately attached to her, that every day she proved her unquestionable superiority over any other female he could know.

In the mornings she continued to attend the Academy.

After having lunch, Jacqueline would spend part of her afternoons in her lover's apartment. They'd decided to read detective novels to refine the details, but to no avail. He'd read a few pages without concentrating; then he'd pick up the newspaper, lay her down next to him, and begin to decipher the political editorials for her, which almost always meant something other than what she assumed. While he read and glossed over the text, she'd unzip his pants, unbutton his shirt, undo his belt, so that when he finished reading, or sometimes before, they'd make love to each other like a pair of feral cats in heat. Jacqueline would try to instill in him some of her hatred for Nicolás Lobato and to make him, outside the act of fornication, think of nothing but the crime. At the same time, she fantasized about the idea of becoming the wife of a future governor, about the wardrobe she'd require, the jewelry she could buy, and—of course!—about the social projects and cultural work she'd undertake. She'd begun, dangerously, to believe in the arguments that she was dispensing to David to strengthen his will. She would appoint, as government advisors, Márgara and Professor Ferraris, who'd surely soften the harshness with which he'd treated her since the day she'd stood him up in Mérida.

Finally, they moved to the house in Polanco. She'd already given up hope of doing so, since the remodeling work had been put on hold so many times. Nicolás wanted to be in charge of everything: the new furniture, the decorating, the movers. The only thing she had to do was pack her bags and move. In the new home she found something she'd always dreamt of: a beautiful studio just for her. She thought it was a good omen: in the times to come, when she became the wife of a prominent politician, that studio would be indispensable to her. She was also happy that they would once again share a bedroom. She'd had enough of separate bedrooms. The move gave her the opportunity to find out where Nicolás kept his pistol and take it. As soon as they arrived at the new house she hid it behind some books, in one of the bookshelves in her study. If Nicolás Lobato tried to defend himself, he wouldn't find the weapon necessary to do so.

When the night arrived, she would find a way to mix three high-dose Valiums into Nicolás's dinner. She planned to state, after the results of the autopsy, that her husband was in the habit of taking sedatives before going to bed, and that she had the impression that he'd been abusing them recently. Days before the move Jacqueline told Elena, the cook, that as soon as they were settled into the new house, she could take her vacation. She thought it would be good if the other servant, the one in charge of the laundry, stayed at home to serve as a witness to the assault that she'd find out about after everything had already happened.

And at last, the longed-awaited moment of liberation arrived. Jacqueline left a bedside lamp on and was reading Choderlos de Laclos's *Dangerous Liaisons*, the book she was studying in her course on novels. She watched as Nicolás fell asleep with his usual ease, perhaps more deeply thanks to the sleeping pill he'd taken. At that moment she got up and opened the door to the garden and the door to the house so that David could enter without difficulty. She would need to give him the signal when it was time to go upstairs to kill her husband. She went back to her room, and—contrary to everything they'd agreed on, and despite the excitement of the moment and the interest with which she was following the novel—she fell asleep. Suddenly she woke up. She saw Nicolás looking for something in a dresser drawer. The pistol! she thought, contorting her face into a sardonic grimace. He approached the bed and whispered to her not to move, not to speak, that apparently someone had entered the house, but that he'd get the drop on them. She closed her eyes; the intensity would only frighten her. She didn't want to know anything, hear anything, see anything. "Let the dead bury their dead!" she murmured, not knowing if it was the right phrase to quote at that moment. She was sure that David would know how to improvise even though something in the plan had changed, that in a few minutes she'd be a widow, and that, even though the circumstances were complex, she was still a good woman, compelled to act as she had only out of love and personal dignity. She was about to repeat to herself the list of affronts she'd been subjected to when she suddenly opened her eyes and saw that Nicolás had taken out, who knows from where, another pistol with a barrel considerably longer than the one she'd taken and was about to leave the room.

Surely Nicolás would catch David Carranza off guard and shoot him or, worse, turn him over to the police. Her lover would spend long years in jail. Perhaps she, too, would be implicated in the trial. She got out of bed in terror: she had to warn the poor boy who was waiting in the room for a signal to go upstairs and finish off the barbarian. She rushed with a heavy vase in her arms towards the staircase in the half-light. She screamed as if driven mad. Nicolás's low voice, asking her to be quiet, guided her towards him and so she was able to smash the vase on his head, but the screams didn't cease:

"Help! Stop, thief! Help! Stop, thief!"

At that moment a shot rang out, and then others. She was unable to tell which pistol they were coming from. Absolute confusion ensued. Terrified to death, she rolled to the ground and clung to one of her husband's legs; then she discovered that she was unable to scream, that she felt a sharp pain in some part of her body that she couldn't pinpoint, she was about to become sick.

When the light came on, she found herself back in a bed in the same hospital. It was daytime. Her hand was bandaged. A nurse told her that she had nothing to worry about, that she'd lost two fingers, but in a few weeks, they would give her even more beautiful ones, her hand would be lovely, she'd soon see, better than before. Nicolás, trying to compose her, added that he had no doubt that they would soon arrest the thief and recover the car. That morning they'd told him at the attorney general's office that they had a letter implicating the culprit, a certain De la Gracia, if his memory didn't fail him. He was under surveillance; they wanted to know how he was connected, but at any moment they would put him behind bars. Jacqueline saw that her husband hadn't been spared altogether either; his head was bandaged.

"I'd never have imagined I had such a fierce wife!" said the imbecile. "But you were mistaken, sister; you hit me, thinking I was the burglar."

Jacqueline's eyes filled with tears. She thought she'd suffered too much: was there any point in going on living? She refused to look at her hand wrapped in an exaggerated bandage.

Two fingers! Which ones were they? Tears streamed down her motionless face, like that of a corpse. She remembered that the night before she'd been reading an interesting book, a novel that was a collection of letters, that she'd heard gunshots, and at that moment she'd fallen asleep.

CHAPTER 4

THE YEAR WAS 1968, MAY to be precise. Jacqueline walked to the window and took a deep breath, convinced that her lungs were filling up with iodine. Four years had passed since she lost her thumb and the index finger on her left hand. Since beginning to wear the prosthesis, Jacqueline had always felt an extreme heaviness in her hand; every movement was clumsy.

"The truth is we all desperately needed this vacation," she said to the cook, whom they'd taken with them. Jacqueline gave her orders that morning in a dry, robotic voice, paying little attention to what she was saying. She ordered her to put the prawns on to boil and, once cooked, to immediately remove their shells; she added that the celery should be cut into small pieces to make a salad, that she should prepare a chicken consommé and put two bottles of white wine in the refrigerator to chill. She then added, again, that she truly, desperately needed this vacation by the sea. She slurred her words, as if pronouncing them cost her great effort. She paced back and forth, repeated again in a chirping voice that it was essential to cut the prawns into small pieces, that she should mix them with the celery, that the salad would be eaten with chilled white wine, although first, of course, the consommé should be served. She opened and closed the refrigerator incessantly until going to stand by the window, as if she didn't want to miss the view of the garden and the sea.

Nicolás had rented, not far from Pie de la Cuesta, a house removed from everything; the doctor had ordered a quiet place, preferably by the sea, lots of mental rest, a little television, and physical exercise.

"My God, what was that? What happened?" she cried out suddenly, her eyes fixed on the clock, "Say something, what was it?" The maid looked at her without the slightest expression on her face. "Please, Elena, stop looking at me like that. I've told you a thousand times not to make me more anxious than I already am. I thought I heard a shot. Did you hear something?" And without waiting for an answer, she ran out of the kitchen, through the dining room, into the garden, and saw her husband, prostrate by the pool. It was two minutes past twelve. Everything had happened as if controlled by a clockwork mechanism. She feigned an expression of surprise, of panic, pain; only to suddenly discover that she wasn't feigning entirely, that her face was awash in tears, that she'd never really hated Nicolás, that it was a monumental mistake, that she could never again look into the eyes of Adolfo—the young, stupid two-bit actor who'd decided to commit this crime. As she knelt beside her husband, she remembered his generosity, his nobility, and at the same time certain unpleasant impulses, the incomprehensible pettiness of the actor with whom she'd been having relations for a little over six months.

Suddenly Nicolás sat up with a surprised expression on his face. At that moment the shot rang out. Jacqueline tried to say something, but the pain overwhelmed her; she didn't even have time to scream before collapsing at Nicolás Lobato's feet, the bullet embedded in her right shoulder.

As if all this weren't already too pathetic, in the hospital in Acapulco, shortly before she was taken to the operating room, as they were giving her a sedative injection, she opened her eyes, looked at her husband and in a faint, perfectly sad voice, murmured:

"So, you've finally managed to get rid of me...?" And she fell asleep.

CHAPTER 5

SINCE HER YEARS AS A university student, she felt an intense hatred for the month of March. The 15th was her birthday. She detested her sign: Pisces, of course. She's often thought that most of the deplorable moments of her life were due to the influence of that ill-fated sign on her destiny.

On March 15, 1974, Jacqueline turned forty-five. At the end of Márgara's class devoted to *The Metamorphosis*, she discovered that the Academy had prepared a surprise party in her honor. Suddenly she noticed at her side the presence of Professor Ferraris, who'd barely spoken to her since that infamous trip to the Yucatán, where she'd met that scatterbrained youth named David Carranza, whom, by the way, she'd not seen again after the failed assassination of Nicolás Lobato. Nor had she heard his name mentioned in the last ten years, nor had she seen him mentioned in the newspapers. It was evident that that boy of sweeping ambitions and negligible brains hadn't achieved the political career he'd dreamt so much about.

Ferraris began to give her a detailed analysis of the Pisces, spoke of their artistic tendencies, their obsessions, their doubtless virtues, their risks, their rewards, and she, who for years had responded to his lack of interest with an equally distant attitude, began, surprised by his sudden burst of eloquence, to be moved. It was true; everything he told her was true. She'd have given her life to be born under the sign of Leo, to be a Taurus woman, strong, determined, implacable. Of course, Jacqueline didn't tell anyone how old she was turning. It was impossible for anyone who saw her to guess her real age. She hadn't neglected herself: massages twice a week, a well-balanced diet, exercise every morning, swimming on Saturdays and Sundays at Las Palmas, hair grafts that truly looked her own. Those who knew her from long before could swear that at thirty-five she stopped aging, and that she looked even better than she did then. She looked around, searching for a mirror, unable to find one. A sudden unease beset her. She had to go to the bathroom to examine her face. There was nothing irregular about it. Then, on her way to the garden, a new wave of sadness swept over her. A feeling of emptiness.

"All these years spent in utter vacuousness!" she murmured. She couldn't understand what she'd done with her life. What had happened to her? Sometimes she thought it would better to have a hole in the center of her hand than the fingers that had been grafted on and moved with excessive difficulty. She'd undergone surgery on her right shoulder. She could write, provided she did it slowly; when eating, no one noticed any clumsiness in her movements. She'd also been operated on for cysts in her most intimate parts. She was certain that the strength on which she prided herself was founded on an unwavering faith in culture. Year after year, she continued to enroll tenaciously in the courses at Márgara Armengol's home. She'd heard over and over about Stendhal, Flaubert, Dostoevsky and Tolstoy, Proust and Kafka, Woolf, Borges, and many other authors whose defining characteristics she wasn't always able to remember precisely. She read the books her teachers discussed in class, but she wasn't what one would call a scholar; for that very reason, if a teacher repeated the same course for two or three years in a row, she hardly noticed it. During each class she'd take notes, fill notebooks, and then put them away in a desk drawer or somewhere else without ever glancing at them again. Her dealings with Márgara Armengol's Academy (and other circumstances related to Nicolás Lobato's economic bonanza), had given her an enviable self-possession. The trips to Europe and New York, which by that time she was able to make almost yearly, her readings, the frequent conversation with worldly and enlightened people, had allowed her to acquire a confidence that she'd lacked until then. Unthinkable as it might seem, her manner of dress had become refined. Her greatest efforts at the Academy were centered on the creative writing workshop. She wrote short stories. The themes were always the same: she'd created a personal universe where the protagonists were usually women like her sisters. She described their petty troubles, their vulgar dreams, the rancor that intoxicated them and spoiled their days every time they mentioned their sister's dazzling success, their sad ambling between bad taste, frustration, and boredom. Jacqueline contemplated those squalid figures from a privileged vantage point. She'd been the only one in her house who'd been able to escape destitution once and for all. Every time María Dorotea and María del Carmen thought they'd emerged from poverty, it was only to return a short time later, to wade in it anew. She wrote on weekends amid the splendor of the palm trees, as Nicolás had built for her a small studio in the garden. Her worktable was next to a large window framed by bougainvillea of varying colors. In the midst of this Eden, she'd slip into the unhappy squalor that surrounded the world her sisters inhabited.

She usually produced a story every ten months, that is, for the duration of the course.

From time to time, she repeated to herself that she adored Nicolás, who at fifty had acquired the air of an imposing victor. The inauguration of his hotel complex was considered at the time a tourist event of national importance. The governor of Morelos, two or three secretaries of state, representatives of the country's financial and most exclusive social circles were present. Nicolás spared no expense. Jacqueline wore a stunning dress bought in New York especially for the occasion, a striking sensation with a plunging neckline, a sheer coral-colored fabric, short in front, with a small train in the back. It was a terrible day. In Cuernavaca, where the rains usually fall at night, there was a sudden gust of wind and then a storm with hail that lasted several hours. Umbrellas were opened to cover the governor, Nicolás, her, and some of the more distinguished guests. Even so, she ended up soaking wet; and because of her light dress she'd spend the next two weeks in bed with a violent fever.

Even if the day of the inauguration had been radiant, that ceremony would have surely pleased her less than the surprise banquet Márgara Armengol hosted to celebrate her birthday. She returned to the garden, where by then her classmates and others from previous years had gathered for the sole purpose of fêting her, as well as the four or five teachers from the Academy. On the terrace they'd prepared a table with finger sandwiches and beverages. Excited, she narrowed her eyes and fell into a hammock; she'd have fallen to the ground had a hand not held her firmly. She felt dizzy, anxious, sad; she remembered that years before, when she still had all her fingers, a palm reader had told her that her emotional equilibrium would be disturbed in a serious way by the future absence of an index and middle fingers. Those weren't exactly the fingers that had been lost in the shooting, but no matter . . . She felt nauseous and wanted to cry and disappear from this world forever. It was an instantaneous sensation. By the time she opened her eyes she'd recovered. At her side, once again, stood Professor Ferraris.

A sudden timidness swept over her. She didn't know what to say; she began to talk to him, lost in an immense daze, about the trip to the Yucatán, about the days that, after their separation in Mérida, she'd spent in Cozumel. Suddenly she extended her wounded hand towards him and showed him the two prosthetic fingers: rigid, discolored. In a neutral voice, like someone who's experienced every kind of horror, she announced:

"The price I paid for my escapade on that cursed island."

"A shark?" he said, puzzled.

"If you like, you can call it that. I had to consult more than one specialist. You shouldn't have allowed me to do anything crazy." She spoke with such intensity that even she was moved. "I've passed from one doctor's hands to another's. I just finished therapy with a psychiatrist, the first one I started with, a return to my origins, so to speak, and now I'm trying to get ahead by my own devices."

It was surely her intuition that led her to follow that course of action. She observed the art professor carefully: he'd changed a great deal since she met him, and she could mention a few additions: a few graying spots on his temples, a neatly trimmed beard, a fixed gaze with a hint of unease. A waiter stopped next to him with a tray of sandwiches, and someone else walked up with the beverages.

"I can only drink soft drinks or fruit juice." And he explained to her at some length that he'd been living on tranquilizers and antidepressants for some time. He learned that Jacqueline had never been prescribed the former, and she didn't even know exactly what they were. "They're the new thing, at least that's what I've been told. You have to lose your fear of chemicals. These are the right drugs to combat anxiety," he added.

"Oh, really?" asked Jacqueline, somewhat frightened, determined to change the subject and, if possible, her seat. It seemed to her that they'd steered the conversation towards topics that were too intimate, and that if they continued along that path, she, as spontaneous as she was, would start talking about the cysts that had been removed from her most intimate parts. She already had so much in life to hide that when it came to topics that weren't specifically dangerous, she was capable of rushing into any topic like a madwoman, without any control whatsoever. But he didn't give her time to retreat and began to tell her some of his misfortunes. He told her that he was the son of Italians, which she already knew, that he'd learned the language of his parents before Spanish, that all his life he'd considered himself an Italian living in Mexico without knowing why. He perfected his language skills at the Italian Institute of Culture, then went on to do a master's degree in Italian literature at the Faculty of Philosophy and Letters; he did most of his reading, of course, in Italian. Was it strange then to imagine that the place where he was supposed to live was Italy?

"I moved to Milan, about four years ago. I suppose you didn't even notice my absence," he said with rancor. I felt like the time had come for me to reside in the country I considered my own and continue my academic life there. A few months later, I discovered that there was no point; the environment in which I was moving was, unfortunately, very mediocre. After a couple of years of seemingly running in place, I decided to return to Mexico; I suddenly realized that, like it or not, Mexico was the only place I knew and where I could do something. In Milan, in any other city in Italy, I'd always be a stranger. I could spend my entire life vegetating there. So, I returned. I returned to the university and resumed my courses at this house of friendship and knowledge created by our dear Márgara. And here I am. Allow me to tell you that the man who returned is different from the one who left with the absurd illusion of taking the world by storm. But Mexico isn't forgiving, my dear friend, not forgiving at all. A few weeks after I returned, I fell victim to a nervous disorder, an inexplicable illness that hasn't given me a moment of peace or mercy since it began. I've been, I swear to you, on the verge of going mad. The first crisis took me unawares: I felt inhabited by a strange, destructive, diabolical force that mocked everything I'd been until that moment and denied me a possibility of change. It was merciless. That night was like an eternity in hell. I knew I was the victim of a dark evil, and what's more I was witness to the possession of a defenseless man. A true split personality, I swear to you. Am I perhaps boring you with these displays of sincerity, with which, I can assure you, I'm not usually so generous?" he asked suddenly in a dry and unpleasant voice. The circles around his eyes were so dark that it gave the impression that he was wearing a mask from whose openings shone a pair of crazed eyes.

"Let me remind you that if anyone understands you here, it's me," Jacqueline replied. "You can't imagine what I've been through . . ."

"Since that night, I've been haunted by terror," continued Ferraris, apparently disinterested in what she'd gone through. "I've seen a psychotherapist who's helped me to live; thanks to him I've come out of the depths of the pit, which is far from implying that I'm completely well. Since then, and perhaps this is the way it should always be, my organism is only being sustained by chemistry. I'm frightened to death at the thought of suddenly stopping my medication, afraid I'll fall hopelessly apart. The fear that the crisis will reappear is constant—the idea that at some totally unexpected moment I could be attacked again by the horror I've suffered won't allow me to live in peace. The early afternoon hours, after lunch, are the worst. What restlessness, mamma mia, what restlessness! In those moments, it feels like an army of ants is running along my nerves, which are already beyond shattered . . ."

He fell silent. Jacqueline didn't know what the appropriate comment should be. She could only gaze at the suffering face and the art teacher's defeated and frightened look. At last, she responded with conviction:

"Call me whenever you feel distressed, no matter the hour, whenever you feel like it. Call your friends. Call me. Perhaps that will help both of us."

And starting that day they began to talk to each other on the phone. Then she decided to visit him, and they began a fertile exchange of tribulations. They spoke at the same time, they didn't understand each other, they just knew they needed each other. Together they went to a curandera for a cleansing. The woman ran eggs over their upper bodies, which she then broke while declaring that each of them, but especially him, had been spat on by the envy of their ill-wishers; they underwent yoga exercises, acupuncture treatments, had tarot and horoscope readings, and the evil began to recede. Almost without realizing it, one day they began to make love, as if it were just another exercise to be used to exorcise the demons that possessed them. The afternoon they undressed for the first time, she was stunned by the foul odor emanating from the teacher's body and the untidiness of his underwear. Unbelievable! That very day she set out to help him correct that anomaly. Her life, Jacqueline thought, had meaning again: she loved and was loved. The first thing she had to do was to restore her lover's self-confidence. One summer Saturday there was a talk by Ferraris on contemporary Italian painting in the lecture hall of Las Palmas. She managed—thanks to the army of employees mobilized by the always-efficient Alicia Villalba, who'd followed Nicolás Lobato to his business in Cuernavaca—to fill the room to capacity. A lavish reception followed. Again, no expense was spared. And at the end, when night fell, when Márgara Armengol's group was about to leave, and Jacqueline was bidding farewell to the guests, possessed by her capacity as a hostess, Ferraris asked her to return with him to the capital. She explained to him, with a wide smile, as if talking to a child, that it was impossible for her to leave Cuernavaca at that hour, that she had to stay with her husband, whom she only saw on weekends, and that Nicolás would never understand if she returned to Mexico City like any another guest.

And that night she surrendered herself to Nicolás Lobato with a frenzy that surprised him again, and that, for a while, would be repeated with the same intensity every weekend.

When she phoned Ferraris the following Monday, a dry, glazed voice replied that he wished to keep as much distance as possible between them, that he couldn't help but feel scorned, he had believed that he was bound to her by a human and not merely animal connection; unfortunately, he'd been mistaken. One more mistake in his stupid, trusting life, he had to admit. She hung up on him, got into her car, and sped off to Calle de la Higuera in

Coyoacán, where her lover's small apartment was located. She knocked on the door for a long while; when he finally opened, she entered like a windstorm, dragging Ferraris with her. She reached the tiny, untidy bedroom, fell like a weight on the bed and burst into tears. A while later, somewhat recovered, she said to him:

"I didn't mean to upset you, Gianni Ferraris. You'll never be able to imagine what my life has been like, you won't be able to understand how I've been able to survive, how I've managed to maintain a glimmer of sanity to this day. You say you've descended into hell, okay, I believe you, but do you think my life the last few years has been a bed of roses? I didn't want to burden you with my misfortunes, I never have, you know, but I think it's necessary that I say something. Do you think it's been easy for me to survive my marriage?" And she began to elaborate, feverishly, on the alleged tortures to which her husband's bestial lechery subjected her. She showed him the hand where the prosthesis had been applied, awkwardly moving her prosthetic fingers, showing him the scar on her shoulder, as if all this were the result of nights of criminal lust; all he could do was stare at her with bulging eyes. "When I met you, I discovered that there were certain things that were no longer accessible to me." And without any transition she spoke of her husband's intellectual and moral limitations, of the offensive opulence in which he vegetated, of his scandalous expenses. She added that on the other hand, for a lecture like Ferraris's and the corresponding reception, he had shown a more than embarrassing miserliness. Ferraris listened to her in astonishment, for he had never in his life attended such a sumptuous event.

That day marked the beginning of the usual refrain: why in hell should Nicolás Lobato enjoy all the gifts of this world when a professor of art history, master of an expansive culture, in need of expensive books and trips to update his knowledge, had to be satisfied with a few crumbs, killing himself in his classes and delivering from time to time lectures before audiences of waiters, hairdressers, and hotel bellboys, who of course had no interest in art? Jacqueline insisted like a cat, hissing her grievances, slipping in at ever convenient moment an insinuation about her husband's unnecessary existence in this world, stressing whenever possible Nicolás's ongoing contempt for art and for any display of culture.

"I don't understand anything," Ferraris would say, whining, "I don't care what your husband thinks or doesn't think. I need peace of mind, don't you see? All I want is peace and you scare me, you torment me. Leave me alone, please, stop distressing me. And as for the lecture you organized in Cuernavaca," he added, wounded, "you never told me what kind of audience I was in front of."

"I didn't want to upset you, Gianni, I couldn't allow myself!" she replied, adding: "If Nicolás were to die, and every night I pray to God that he does, I'd immediately sell Las Palmas, that pharaonic hotel that I detest so much. That would solve our problems for the rest of our lives."

After these conversations, Ferraris's nervous breakdowns began to manifest themselves with unusual violence. Everything he'd gained in the previous weeks was instantly lost. He'd lie on the bed, writhe, rub his arms and chest. The ants under his skin were crawling all over his body. He was visibly losing weight. But Jacqueline's words had managed to inject their poison. If Lobato died, he could recover his health in one of the best clinics in the world, in the Swiss Alps, in the Black Forest, in Málaga. He dreamt of himself in a room in the Alps leafing through a luxurious monograph by Giorgio Morandi sent from Italy so that he could write an essay while he underwent the appropriate treatment.

"And is there any chance, dare I say any hope, that your husband might die soon? Does he have any health problems?" he finally asked one day.

"Nicolás Lobato is an oak, or at least he thinks he is, but I'll be the one to bring him down. The time has come to repay him with evil for all the evil he's done to me over the years. Let me think for a while about how we'd have to eliminate him. We could drug him with a sleeping pill, for example, put him in a car, take him to a mountain road on the way to Cuernavaca, and once there hurl his car over a cliff. Death—I imagine, I hope—would be instantaneous. I could drive his car; we would go along the old road so as not to be stopped at the toll booths. I'd wear a raincoat I bought some years ago in London, a beautiful raincoat, not just any raincoat, I assure you," she said in a fit of incoherence, and then continued, "I'd stop the car at the edge of a cliff, get out, and then you, with the other car, would give it a little push. That would be enough. We would hurry back to my house to wait for the phone call that would announce that everything was over, that our limitless oppression was a mere matter of the past, that the most radiant future was opening its arms to welcome us like its favorite children."

Gianni Ferraris never gave his approval to these schemes; however, he allowed himself to be manipulated like an automaton, as if he were unable to escape from a dream. They made several trips to pick the appropriate site and thought of the best way to attract Nicolás Lobato to Mexico City, where he might not set foot for weeks at a time. Jacqueline repeated, with an intense sensation of déjà vu, one of the plots she'd devised in the past. She would pretend to be sick, telephone Cuernavaca as if she were dying. It would have to be on a Saturday afternoon or in the evening. On

Sunday there would be no one at home, they would load Nicolás's drug-saturated body into a car and carry out the grand operation.

Ferraris had to take very strong doses of tranquilizers during those days; his reactions grew slower every day, his language more slurred. Jacqueline wanted the accident to happen as soon as possible, fearing that a long wait could be fatal for her lover. It was clear to her that her project was still in an embryonic state, that the details were barely outlined, still being worked out, but she was confident that everything would be resolved by the intuition of the moment. If she didn't act soon, Gianni would eventually crack, end up in a psychiatric hospital. At that point in their relationship, his organism was so battered that they could no longer make love; on the other hand, the weekends she spent with her husband reached orgiastic, maddening extremes, as happened every time she plotted his death.

In the end they decided on an exact date; Jacqueline again took her lover to study the chosen site. That night they would dine at her home with Márgara Armengol and a French lover who accompanied her everywhere—a disagreeable type who had the insufferable habit of talking a blue streak. As was usual in Jacqueline's life, things happened in a dramatic way, but in a completely different way than she'd anticipated.

That evening, while dining with Márgara and her chatty friend, two police officers suddenly appeared in Jacqueline's dining room. They asked in a peremptory tone for Nicolás Lobato, and as was natural she answered with a certain inconstancy that he wasn't at home and that he rarely dined there, for the simple reason that he'd moved the bulk of his business to Cuernavaca; her husband was the owner, in case they didn't know, of the hotel complex Las Palmas, a place so important that it even had a golf course. When the kitchen door opened, she could see that other agents had also entered the house and were questioning the servants. One of them, who seemed to hold a higher rank, insulted Márgara and the Frenchman rudely, for trying to interrupt the investigation with their presence, and ordered them to leave the house at that very moment with the condition that they not leave the city until they received written authorization to do so. Jacqueline was thunderstruck. For a moment she was overcome with the hope that her husband was no longer inhabiting the realm of the living without her and Ferraris having to sully their hands. As soon as Márgara and her friend left the house, the interrogation took on a different tone. Jacqueline and Ferraris were insulted with the foulest words imaginable. She had the feeling that the agents took it for granted that Gianni was her lover. They insisted on knowing where her husband was, where in the hell they'd hidden him, when they'd last seen him, what time he'd phoned that day and from where. They didn't want to treat them with the harshness their silence deserved, one of them said, as he delivered a monumental slap to Ferraris in the face, still demanding clear and truthful answers. Where was Nicolás Lobato hiding? Where had he escaped to? Then came the threats. If they didn't sing—said the one with the fast hand, while shaking Jacqueline violently by the shoulders—they'd be thrown in jail, have their heads stuck in buckets full of shit, and her faggot horndog would be strung up by his balls. They'd see if they continued to play dumb when they felt a pair of boots dancing mambo on their precious bellies; when they left them without a single unbroken bone, they'd see . . . they'd see . . .

"What happened to my husband?" asked Jacqueline, fearful and now completely disoriented. "Tell me at once, I beg you."

"Will you give me your ass as a prize if I tell you? Look, little miss pissypants, we ask the questions here, and the sooner you learn that, the better," answered one of the officers obscenely, giving Ferraris another slap to the face. Then the room filled with policemen and Ferraris began to emit incoherent screams, thrashing his arms like windmill blades, and one of the policemen twisted his wrists behind his back, and the screams began to turn into groans; his whole body trembled wildly, while the officers began to tear the house apart in search of something that Jacqueline couldn't figure out what it was. The contents of drawers and filing cabinets lay in disarray on the floor. Soon after, the couple was loaded into a police car and left for the unknown.

Jacqueline was held for almost two weeks. During the interrogations she learned that her husband had gone bankrupt, according to the police, knowingly and fraudulently, and disappeared from his Morelos complex. They treated her as if she were a criminal of the worst sort, they insulted her, shook her, pulled her hair, they wanted to know where she'd hidden her husband's body. Night and day, they asked her the same questions repeatedly. She knew nothing and therefore could answer nothing. When they finally released her, she looked for Ferraris and discovered that he'd not yet returned to his apartment. Worse than the rigors of prison for her was reading the press. From the newspapers she learned that she and the art teacher were suspected of having committed a crime; specifically, of having murdered Nicolás Lobato on the old highway to Cuernavaca. Ferraris had possibly talked about their plan and the police assumed that the crime had already taken place. In any case, Ferraris had declared that his confession was invalid since it had been extracted from him by means of torture.

It sickened her to read the press, where she was treated with unparalleled commonness. The only thing left to do was to find the corpse, the journalists maintained. There were days when she thought she was about to go mad. Her siblings showed no sign of life, for which she was grateful; the maids had abandoned her, even before she returned home, surely frightened by the police. Márgara Armengol refused to take her calls; when, unawares, she picked up the receiver, recognizing Jacqueline's muffled voice, she immediately hung up. The house had been the victim of a general looting; her furs, her jewelry, the silver, everything was gone. Poor Gianni was still under arrest, and she wasn't allowed to visit him. The only support she found was in Alicia Villalba, who'd taken the steps necessary to free her; she'd also put her in contact with Nicolás Lobato's attorney, a certain Licenciado Paredes—Marcelino Paredes, to be exact. Months later, that same Licenciado Paredes was able to present reliable proof that Nicolás Lobato was perfectly alive and that he was in Madrid, from where he couldn't be extradited because there was no treaty between Mexico and Spain.

It took several more months for the documentation apostilled by the Mexican consular office in Madrid to arrive, which confirmed without question Nicolás Lobato's presence in Spain. And it was thanks to these documents that it was possible to obtain Gianni Ferraris's freedom.

One morning there was a knock at Jacqueline's door. She got up to open it, sure that it was Alicia Villalba. However, it was Gianni Ferraris who came in. When she opened the door, she noticed a repulsive stench on the teacher's breath, which immediately gave her a bad feeling. He was furious, but he didn't speak, didn't shout, as he'd have done in the past. He dragged her into the bedroom, placed her in a corner, backed up a little, then ran at her with his head down and rammed her in the chest, making her lose her balance and roll to the floor. Then he continued to beat her brutally, maniacally.

It was unbelievable how much strength that man had acquired in the state of semi-dementia he was in. Jacqueline didn't know how long the attack lasted, nor at what time the Italian left her house. She awoke many hours later with her body full of bruises. The room was dark. She could barely get up and look for the light switch. She walked to the bed as if asleep. When she saw herself in the full-length mirror she was terrified by her appearance, her face covered with bruises, her clothes bloody and torn, one of her shoes missing. She decided to call a doctor, but all her strength would allow her to do was get to the bed, where she lost consciousness again.

CHAPTER 6

IT WAS FORTUNATE THAT THE house was deeded in her name. At least she had somewhere to take refuge. Licenciado Paredes suggested that she get rid of it and, with the money she received, buy an apartment that another client was about to put up for sale in Colonia Nápoles.

"You'll be halfway between Coyoacán and Polanco, the two places where you've lived up to now," the attorney commented, as if being in-between might ease the suffering and panic that had taken hold of her!

The money, Paredes insisted, should be deposited immediately in a bank account in order to preserve the capital and live off the interest. However, she wasn't able to buy the apartment in Nápoles, as the sale of her house took longer than expected. On several occasions, Nicolás presented her with documents to sign, which she always did in a mechanical fashion, never asking what they were, confident in her husband's business acumen. When she ready to sell, it turned out that the Polanco house was saddled with a hefty mortgage. Only after a series of cumbersome and, what seemed to her, incomprehensible formalities that took more than a year to resolve, during some of which a notary showed her papers signed in her own handwriting, of which she had no recollection, was Licenciado Paredes able to carry out the transaction and obtain a ridiculous sum for the house where she'd been so unhappy. An employee of the attorney oversaw the sale of the furniture, for which she also received a pittance.

And one day she found herself living in a small, shabbily furnished apartment on Calle Balderas. And, so, she hadn't escaped the fate of her relatives; she, too, was wading in poverty. She lived on the meager interest that the bank doled out to her, but she was determined, for the first time since her wedding day, to be vigilant with her money. Since her relocation to Calle Balderas, she could do nothing but play solitaire and ruminate obsessively on her past. Life to her was like an aimless journey through the desert. Deep down, she told herself, despite what appearances might indicate, her path had known very little variation. The most serious problem in her immediate future didn't seem economic, but rather the immense loneliness that was fencing her in. She didn't feel able to ask any of Lobato's friends for help. The press had treated her so mercilessly that she took it for granted that she'd be expelled from wherever she went. Turning to her relatives was something she'd never even have thought of, and she'd never give María Dorotea a pleasure of such magnitude! Her staunchest emotional pillar, apart from her marital and extra-marital relationships, had been for many years her friendship with Márgara Armengol. She was sure that the feeling was reciprocal. Time would take care of resolving the misunderstandings that had arisen between them. The moment would come when Márgara would need her as intensely as she needed Márgara. They would talk as if nothing had happened. Thinking of Márgara carried her back to her blissful years as a student, to her courtship with Nicolás Lobato, to her marriage and to the many vicissitudes of married life. Through Márgara she'd passed through the gateway to the world of culture. Their friendship gave unity to her life. Thinking of Márgara meant reliving the nights spent preparing for exams with Benzedrine, the parties of adolescence, Cuba libres, Smirnoff vodka, cheap gin, the respective and unbearable hangovers, staying up until dawn dancing the mambo and the chachachá. An appearance of unyielding chaos and, deep down, absolute innocence! Then, the birth of new aspirations: art galleries, film clubs, classes, whole years cultivating herself to be a woman whom her husband couldn't demean whenever he felt like it. What good did it do her! She knew very well that, with her mother dead, her true family wasn't made up of María del Carmen, María Dorotea, Adrián, or Marcelo, but of Márgara and a handful of other people from that circle. For that reason, she looked to her before anyone else when she got out of jail. With discouraging results, as we already know.

When she thought that enough time had passed for Márgara to recover from her initial shock, she phoned again. Her friend accepted the call, and Jacqueline greeted her with a titanic effort, trying to adopt a tone if not nonchalant at least with some semblance of normality. In the first anxious moment of uncertainty, she thought her friend would hang up on her. But apparently Márgara Armengol had decided to establish her position definitively: she remained silent at first, until Jacqueline, increasingly hesitant, finally asked if she was listening to her. At that moment, in a cold, steely voice, the person on the other end said that she was demanding, not begging, not requesting, but, she emphasized, demanding that she suspend all contact with her and also with the teachers and students of her Academy. She told her tremendously unpleasant things about the facts she'd learned from the press, especially about the relations she'd had with one of the teachers at her institution, as if she'd never, she later said to herself—despite the fact that for years she'd been her most intimate confidant!—noticed that her ties with Ferraris were more intimate than those that a pupil normally establishes with a teacher. She also stated that the press had informed her of other situations, the sordidness of which she would never have dared to imagine, such as the plan to assassinate her husband, in which, with obvious bad faith, she'd tried to implicate the aforementioned Professor Ferraris.

"Allow me to say," she continued, switching from the familiar to the formal address, "that it's perhaps more painful for me than for you to speak of these facts. I could never have suspected that you would reciprocate with such behavior the courtesies that I and my staff extended to you during the time your presence was tolerated in this institution of culture. And that is all!" she concluded abruptly, hanging up the receiver.

For Jacqueline the blow was terrible.

The period that followed was the most desolate she'd ever known.

It would be useful to review some previous events to better understand this story:

When Jacqueline came to following the concussion produced by the blows delivered by Gianni Ferraris, she stood up in excruciating pain, feeling that she was once again on the brink of losing consciousness; she managed to throw a coat over herself and leave the house. She didn't know how long she'd been unconscious. She didn't even wash her face; the cuts had left scabs of dried blood that, together with the bruises produced by burst blood vessels, disfigured her hideously. The woman, with slow and uncertain steps, wandered for a time through the streets in search of a cab, an immense sack of pains. From her doctor's office she was immediately sent to a hospital, where she remained for about two weeks. Apart from a visit from Alicia Villalba, she remained there completely forgotten. She was placed in a surgical corset, given stitches in an open wound above her right eyebrow, several daily injections, and made to take sedatives at all hours. From the sanatorium she telephoned Paredes's office several times, who never came to the phone or returned her calls. Once she was discharged, Jacqueline went to visit him straightaway. The attorney apologized with a dismissiveness that bordered on incivility. He commented that her messages had never been passed on to him, but that he didn't think it was worth arguing about past mistakes. It was then that he assured her that she had the right to keep the house in Polanco, since it was deeded in her name, and suggested that she put it up for sale and move to a less expensive place. He added that the two cars had to be turned over to a representative of the creditors as they were in Lobato's name.

Jacqueline asked the attorney for her husband's address in Spain; it was urgent, she said, that she contact him to ask for instructions. Should she sell everything and meet him somewhere in Spain? She still knew nothing at that time about the lien on the property, and how little she'd receive from the sale of a mortgaged house. The attorney refused to provide her with the requested address. He would need to consult with his client first, he said. Jacqueline was shocked. There and then she wrote a letter and gave it to Paredes, with the plea that he forward it to her husband. In it she told her husband that she'd been arrested, harassed, and slandered, and that she was haunted by the belief that the scandal had forever sullied her life. An Italian professor named Ferraris, she didn't know if he'd remember him, had been forced through torture to confess to the existence of a plot to murder him, yes, him, Nicolás Lobato, to seize his fortune, and who due to the harshness of the treatment he'd received had ended up losing his mind; that later he'd been found innocent and released from jail, and that during one of his usual fits of madness had assaulted her with criminal violence, the consequences of which left her far from completely healed. In that letter she gently asked him for some financial help, a monthly pension, to help her cope with her difficult situation until she could sell the house and be reunited with him.

She never received a reply to that letter. During the ensuing months she saw the attorney again who oversaw the sale of the mortgaged house, as well as the furniture, for which, as has been said, she received an amount far below their real value, but which allowed her to move into the apartment on Calle Balderas. As with other circumstances of her life, her movements and the events themselves seemed to unfold in a dreamlike landscape, where she was at once the protagonist and a witness who recorded and judged everything that happened. It was better this way, to not comprehend the magnitude of her despair, of the barren future that awaited her. Little by little, without fully appreciating the process, she began to register reality again. She didn't have a clear understanding of the time that had elapsed during that period. Was she still living in the house in Polanco, or had she already moved to the modest place on Balderas? During the first months of recovery from reality, she spent most of the time shut away, trying to read some of the works she'd studied at the Academy, which she hadn't looked at since she'd been in prison. From time to time, she was overcome with bouts of melancholy, almost always foretold by an acute nervous disequilibrium. "The last thing I needed," she mumbled, "was to suffer the crawling sensation that damn lunatic complained about so much," and on those days she closed her books and lay in bed, taking the medication that a neurologist, recently recommended by Dr. Montenegro, her doctor, had prescribed for her. She could spend weeks at a time doing nothing but playing solitaire.

When she realized that too much time had passed since she'd had news from Nicolás Lobato, she made a new effort to solve her problems herself. She dressed as austerely as possible and returned to the office of the elusive Paredes; she asked him for a recommendation for a job; but the attorney, without refusing entirely, didn't give her one either. As usual, he said he'd have to request—she could understand better than anyone else—permission from his client. Jacqueline replied that she understood his reservations, but she'd be very grateful to him if he'd inform Nicolás, when he got in touch with him, that she'd been arrested, tortured physically and morally, excoriated mercilessly in the press, treated like the worst sort of woman, like a vile whore, assaulted by a madman, and that more than once believed she was also on the verge of going mad; that, regardless, she'd endured those difficult trials out of solidarity with him, out of affection, that is to say, out of love, that he also tell him that she'd moved to a very modest apartment at Balderas 95, 6 interior, requesting that he please send her a few lines to that address with the necessary instructions on what she should do in the future, whether to move to Spain or to wait for him in Mexico.

The same: she never received a single line from Nicolás Lobato. She lived for a year in the Balderas apartment, bored, without finding the slightest meaning to her days, having lost the desire to read, without friends, alone, except for the occasional visit from Alicia Villalba, or from an elderly neighbor, a talkative and generous medium. By then, Jacqueline had stopped reading; it was impossible for her to concentrate. She was unable to become interested in anything. Opening a book produced a new sadness in her, it distressed her, because it forced her to confront her disabilities. It was her kind-hearted neighbor who introduced her to Mario and Manuel Requena, her nephews, who ran a business selling esoteric books next to the Metropólitan movie theater; both read tarot cards and did horoscopes. They offered her a job, which she accepted since the bookstore was only three blocks from her building and traveling long distances had become a source of panic. Nothing would have made her visit Polanco, where until recently she'd still lived, much less the neighborhood of Coyoacán, where she'd spent most of her life, and where, among other links with her past, Márgara Armengol's Academy was located. She recognized that if she hadn't taken that job, she'd have begun to die little by little, and might have ended up committing suicide. The bookstore brought her back to life. Mario Requena approached her one day to tell her that the business was doing so well that the time had come to open a branch in Cuernavaca. He'd been offered a very suitable location a stone's throw from the Casino de la Selva, El Zodíaco; a café perfectly suited to install a branch of his esoteric establishment. He was leaving not because of disagreements with his brother, but for health concerns; the altitude of Mexico City was bad for him, his heart had already given him a couple of warnings, and she, who didn't even dare so much as to stray a few blocks from her apartment or the bookstore, accepted with delight, to her own surprise, the proposal that Mario then made to her, and settled in a tiny little house next to El Zodíaco. She lived there for the next ten years, without feeling them, without living them completely. She learned the most rudimentary elements of the coded language of her new environment. Mario Requena tried to teach her with the help of a manual to read the lines of the hand, but she did it without conviction, in a voice that failed to transmit the appropriate emanations, nor did it create any expectation of mystery, so her teacher thought it prudent to ask her to give up her career as a palm reader. In her leisure time she read, without understanding a line, fragments of esoteric books that entertained her in an inexplicable way, but from which she wouldn't have been able to repeat a single word later. On one occasion, shortly after her arrival in Cuernavaca, the cards told her that she'd already lived three different lives and that she'd have to live two more so that the pentagram of her existence would close in a natural way and the chords of all that she'd lived until then could merge into the melody that was destined for her astrally.

"What? I've already lived three times?" Jacqueline asked, without hiding her astonishment.

"What isn't clear to me," Requena responded, "is whether it's a matter of three different lives that have taken place within the same person, or whether it refers to three persons that make up a single life."

"Is it not perhaps the same thing?" she asked, even more perplexed.

"So obscure are the arcana of life!" Requena concluded in the voice of a seer.

Jacqueline decided not to have her tarot read any more, because the results distressed her too much. She contemplated with discouragement her three known lives: first, her poor childhood, sordid adolescence, university years, the miracles performed to be able to show up with a modicum of neatness at the faculty; the second, beginning with her marriage and its culmination, was marked not only by the loss of a house in Polanco, where, among other things, a butler served her cereal for breakfast with white gloves, but also that of a rich intellectual atmosphere that included the courses at Márgara Armengol's home, her readings, the short stories she wrote and which remained unpublished, her dealings with writers and intellectuals of the most diverse sort, who were guests periodically at the Academy, an atmosphere much more attractive than the one in which her husband moved, whatever he might say; and the third, which began with the flight of Nicolás Lobato and his inexplicable silence, followed by her plunge into poverty, exile in Cuernavaca, where she lived with only one servant and most of the time without one altogether, without caring what she ate or how she dressed, only surviving, as if that were the only goal she was allowed. She was unable to find any thread linking these three different stages of her existence; even between the last two, the most recent ones, the nexuses were scarce, the most visible being her dealings with Alicia Villalba, who after Nicolás's economic collapse had remained in Cuernavaca, of course not at Las Palmas, but as the manager, and later also as a partner, of a French restaurant where she was doing very well. Nicolás's cousin had been extremely generous with her, to the point of lending her a car that she barely drove, so that she could get around Cuernavaca. Jacqueline often talked on the phone with Alicia and the few acquaintances she had in the city, all of them clients of El Zodíaco, one of the few resources she had to conceal her loneliness. She loved to listen to her husband's former secretary don an affected voice and put on airs as she talked about her problems at the restaurant, those with the employees, with the suppliers, with the clients, with Sara, her associate, the woman with whom she'd been living since she moved to Cuernavaca, a corpulent and eternally cheerful Frenchwoman, which didn't prevent her from being forever ready to contradict Alicia in public. Jacqueline rarely intervened in the telephone conversations, but listening to another voice for a little while lessened the anxiety that the medications weren't always able to alleviate completely.

Alicia Villalba ventured to El Zodíaco every two or three months to consult her horoscope and then take Jacqueline out to have dinner at a nice place, because she considered it a professional obligation to frequent the city's restaurants, to know what was new, to do public relations, and to enhance her media presence. And she was self-confident enough not to worry about appearing in public next to a fat, prematurely aging woman, with a bewildered air, thin, unkempt hair, chubby hands with gnawed fingernails, festooned in a tunic so graceless that rather than a dress it looked like the habit of a penitent nun who was fulfilling a religious commandment. On those occasions, when Jacqueline had the rare opportunity to interrupt one of the restaurateur's long soliloquies, it wasn't to talk about alchemy, palmistry, or tarot, as her friend wished, but to repeat once again the horrific experience of being arrested, locked in a cell, where she spent the first two days next to a humble-looking criminal who frightened her to death with the stories of her captivity, only to move on to the interrogations to which she was subjected, her tremendous mistake in befriending a clearly unbalanced Italian, a mythomaniac who confessed to hair-raising things, perhaps under pressure from who knows what acts of torture, or perhaps because of the dementia he'd already shown on several occasions, always ending up referring to Nicolás Lobato's long and inexplicable silence, and at that point sighing deeply, shedding a few tears, and hastily drinking two cups of chamomile tea.

And precisely on the thirteenth of March she received a call from Alicia Villalba. She was going to El Zodíaco in a couple of days, she wanted to ask her for an appointment with Mario Requena, although, she added, she wasn't just calling her for that, but to beg her to go that day to the beauty salon to do herself up and put on her best outfit, because after the session she'd take her to L'Aiglon to celebrate her birthday. It would be just the two of them; Sara, her friend, had gone to spend a few days in Cozumel with her parents. Jacqueline sighed. On the fifteenth she'd be sixty years old.

She bought some costume-jewelry necklaces and others with brightly colored ceramic beads; she went to the hairdresser, put on a champagne-colored dress, which a local seamstress had altered so that it would fit comfortably; fortunately, it wasn't too old-fashioned; she was surprised herself at the results when she saw herself in the mirror. Ever since Alicia had arrived at El Zodíaco, Jacqueline picked up on something unusual about her: her greeting, for example, had been an ambiguous gesture, triumphant and complicit at the same time, to the extent that she came to think that that night her friend intended to confide something in her, perhaps talk to her about a romantic problem between her and the French woman, instead of entertaining herself as usual talking about her problems with suppliers and cooks, the tax authorities, the regular patrons, the waiters and the union, and that saddened her, just as any announcement of change had saddened her in recent times. She'd imagined everything except what she was going to learn that night. Alicia Villalba began by scolding her, because even on that occasion she wouldn't agree to have a glass of wine; Jacqueline was adamant, not daring to disobey her doctor's order not to mix alcohol with her tranquilizers. Alicia insisted on how special this day was and toasted with a dry Campari while Jacqueline toasted with a glass of mineral water. When Alicia asked whether the cards had predicted any good news for her, she reminded her that since her arrival in Cuernavaca she'd only had her fortune told once, soon after arriving. She became so disconcerted on that occasion that she preferred to discover her destiny on her own and not by means that deep down caused her dread.

"If you had," Alicia told her, "you wouldn't be surprised to learn that Nicolás Lobato has returned to Mexico. He's in Veracruz, where he's decided to live. It seems that his high blood pressure is preventing him from going up to the capital. He came back with all his legal affairs in order. He's opened a hardware store in the port. What do you think? I imagine you'll be interested to know that he hasn't remarried."

Jacqueline remained silent for a good while, staring at her hostess. She took a piece of bread, buttered it, sprinkled salt on it, and began to eat it with excessive deliberateness. At a certain moment she paused to say in a voice that didn't express the slightest emotion:

"I find it hard to believe that he would marry." And with great effort, between mouthfuls of buttered bread and with visible reluctance, she managed to express that he couldn't, for the simple reason that he'd never divorced her.

As if Alicia knew the rest of the argument, she interrupted the birthday girl:

"Jacqueline, dear, when a man sets his mind to it, he can be the biggest bastard in the world. He can divorce you behind your back, so that you'll be the last to know that you've lost your husband. I don't know if Nicolás is divorced or not; all I know is that he arrived alone in Veracruz. That's all. I wanted to be the one to tell you the news." There was a pause, which she interrupted to say, "It may seem strange to you, but I must confess that I stopped believing in youth a long time ago." Alicia Villalba's complexion was magnificent. Her face, increasingly masculine, showed none of the ravages of time, which wasn't the case with her guest. "Do you want me to tell you something else today since you've found me in the mood for confidences? I'm more than convinced that life begins at sixty. And if I'm not mistaken, Nicolás turns sixty this year."

"That's next year," Jacqueline hastened to correct, remembering that her husband was a year younger than she. "How did you find out that he's back in the country?"

"A little birdie told me, a friend of mine, tweet, tweet! He just came back! Before he arrived, a proxy of some sort, perhaps a partner, had already opened a hardware store in the center of Veracruz, two blocks from the Diligencias Hotel. See for yourself" She handed her a card, where she'd written the name of Nicolás Lobato, and below that *Ferretería Moderna*, and the address in Veracruz. Alicia Villalba looked at Jacqueline with something akin to astonishment, and she didn't ask anything else, she didn't mention Nicolás or their separation or a possible meeting.

They ate the consommé. Then the waiter served them the chateaubriand with legumes. The menu was always decided by the proprietrix, who had the impression that her guest's obesity was due to an excess of flour and a lack of meat. Jacqueline spent a long time engaged in cutting her meat into very small pieces, which she then ate as slowly as possible, with such a blank expression on her face that one might have thought she was inebriated. Alicia believed that the news had disturbed her, that it should have been administered to her gradually, that surely all she could do was think of Nicolás. So she was very surprised when her friend, halfway through her course, began to talk, and that her conversation had no connection with the news she'd received, but rather referred entirely to the fateful days of her detention: to the rancid swill they passed off as food, to the interrogations that lasted entire nights, carried out in a narrow room illuminated by a blaring spotlight, so that she never knew whether it was day or night; to the campaign of slander of which she'd been the victim; to the crazed declarations of the professor of art history, the baneful Ferraris, which the press reproduced in lurid detail. That day she expanded the story to an area she'd never touched on before—to the beating that the crazed Italian had visited on her as soon as he was released, and from which she'd never been able to recover psychologically. Then she said that she felt very tired, that she could no longer resist her drowsiness, and asked her to please call her a cab.

Alicia insisted that she stay a while longer, she had to try the blackberry cake that she'd ordered in her honor, but Jacqueline was obstinate about leaving. Upon noticing her prostration, the hostess asked the chauffeur to take her in her car.

In the car, Jacqueline burst into tears and continued crying at home for most of the night. On more than one occasion she got up to sit in front of the mirror and tell herself that the only man she'd ever loved and respected was Nicolás Lobato, and that ever since the moment he'd abandoned her, her existence had been meaningless.

She was able to sleep for three hours at most. The next morning, after bathing and taking breakfast, about to leave for El Zodíaco, she suddenly changed her mind, went back to her room, hurriedly packed a suitcase, put it in the car and left for

Mexico City. She stopped there only to fill up with gas. At about six o'clock in the evening she parked her car in Veracruz, next to the Ferretería Moderna.

Dead tired, semi-conscious, battered by the trip, Jacqueline entered the hardware store in a somnambulistic state. Before she realized it, she was standing in front of Nicolás Lobato. She saw a tall man, with a broad back, on the plump side, but not exactly fat. Everything about him was smiling, his lips, his eyes, his skin. "You can tell he's a happy man from a mile away," she said to herself. At the same time, despite the well-being he emanated, she could also see that during the years of his absence, Nicolás had lost the youthful appearance he'd preserved until the day of his disappearance. He too had aged. He was a content man, but old. He looked at her with a certain blankness, and when he finally recognized her, neither of them knew what to say. Jacqueline held out her hand and looked away. Nicolás Lobato opened the counter flap, walked through, and embraced her as one embraces a sister. Then he gave a few orders to his employees. He wouldn't return that night to close. He asked Jacqueline for her luggage and led her to the hotel where he was staying.

She thought they would spend the night talking, but they didn't. They discussed only part of what had happened during the years of separation. She learned that Licenciado Paredes had sent her husband the newspaper articles that had appeared during her arrest, that he'd come to believe what they said about her love affair with Ferraris, although, of course, he hadn't given credence to the statements concerning the plot to assassinate him. What madness! He chattered on that his high blood pressure had convinced him to return to Mexico, not wanting to die anywhere else; that his debts were entirely paid off; that his dream,

Las Palmas, was beyond his means, but that it had been worth living for, although fate, the sole repository of truth, had determined his stature, forcing him to live out his days in a hardware store, just as he'd started; that the years abroad had taught him a lesson, that of accepting the facts as they were; that life in the port was quite pleasant; that in a couple of months they'd be handing over a house he'd already rented, with an option to buy; for the moment, it was still under construction. She thought it would soon be her turn to talk, but as soon as Nicolás referred to the house, he turned his back on her and fell asleep.

The sun awakened them very early. Almost without a word, they bathed, dressed, and went downstairs for breakfast. She felt ashamed for having neglected herself so much in the last few years. She paused for a moment in front of the mirror: she saw a fat, haggard witch. She told him that she'd moved to Cuernavaca, where she got a job that allowed her to support herself. Living in that city made her feel close to him, thanks to which she'd saved her life; of the building where she lived in Mexico City, only the foundation was left. The earthquake had reduced it to rubble. After breakfast, Nicolás took her to a jewelry store and there he bought two wedding rings; he took her hand and placed one on her ring finger, next to the old ring she'd never parted with. Then he put the other on his own hand.

"No more talking about it! What each of us has lived through during these years is a thing of the past! These wedding rings erase everything!" exclaimed Nicolás with a thick Spanish accent that, for all its parody, made it easier for each of them to adapt to the new situation. Jacqueline remembered the tarot reading she'd done upon arriving in Cuernavaca and wondered if this conjugal reunion would finally complete the pentagram that governed her existence. And at that moment she remembered that, if she wasn't mistaken, the fourth phase of her life was beginning and that she was missing one last one for the pentagram to be completed.

Once in the car, Nicolás took her on a tour of Boca del Río, making a series of banal comments about the places they passed, as if she didn't know Veracruz. On the way back, at Villa del Mar, he turned right and drove three or four blocks until stopping in front of a house where some bricklayers were working on the roof. He showed it to her with a wide gesture.

"Your house?"

"That's right, milady! This is the house! In two months at the latest we'll be able to move in. Well," he added in a brisk tone, "I've got to fly to the hardware store. I'll pick you up at the hotel at two o'clock in the afternoon so we can have lunch together."

She found the commanding voice with which Nicolás Lobato gave her instructions pleasant, but when she arrived at the hotel, she looked at herself again in the mirror and couldn't hide the revulsion that her appearance produced in her. She cursed Cuernavaca. That repugnant place had transformed her into a cow. She had to start immediately to reclaim her body. Nothing better than a swim in the sea! She requested a call to Cuernavaca. They put her through immediately. She told Alicia Villalba everything that had happened. She told her that she'd be staying in Veracruz and asked her to please send someone to deal with her house and take care of the few things she had, until she was able to give her the address where she could send them. She lay down on the bed, but sleep was impossible. She left her room, got into the car, and began to drive around Veracruz. At one point she felt like stepping on the accelerator and not stopping until she reached the café-bookstore El Zodíaco. She felt unworthy, she'd turned her life into a mess. During the thirty-odd years of her marriage to Nicolás Lobato she'd made nothing but foolish mistakes. She bought some newspapers and magazines and locked herself in her room again; then she returned downstairs to buy a notebook and a fountain pen to try to write a chronicle of her courtship and the first years of her marriage. She seemed to have forgotten everything she'd learned in the creative writing workshop. She tried several times to describe the distant time when they were students, the night Nicolás took her to a burlesque theater to see Kalantán dance, but she was unable to progress more than half a page, each line dotted with deletions. Everything in her prose seemed deficient, meager. She went back downstairs. She had a cup of coffee and suddenly realized it was five after two in the afternoon, and she wasn't sure if Nicolás would pick her up or if she was the one who should pick him up at the hardware store. She didn't have the phone number. She looked it up in the directory but didn't find the name of the hardware store listed, as it was apparently too new. She went up to her room and came down again; at last, when she was about to go out to look for her husband, she saw him approach, glowing, animated, and she felt that she was about to become a bundle of nerves, on the verge of passing out. She was afraid to cry in public, but was luckily able to contain herself this time.

They ate at Prendes. Then they went to one of the cantinas along the same portico to have a coffee and a drink. Jacqueline came to feel that the years hadn't passed. Far from the governors, bankers, and other important people, Nicolás had somehow returned to being the simple and friendly law student of forty years before. That day, for the first time since she began taking antidepressants, she dared to have a glass of brandy with her coffee. The effect of the liquor, the music of the marimba, the restless coming and going of people between tables, the atmosphere of collective jubilation, had achieved a miracle: her eyes were animated again. She gazed ecstatically at Nicolás. Between her half-opened eyelids, a languid gaze expressed the pleasure of the reunion.

A foreign language suddenly reached them. A group of young sailors were speaking Portuguese at the next table. Jacqueline began to enjoy the musicality of their voices, the counterpoint of the virile, playful, and plebeian accents of those who spoke that language. She stared at the group with fascination. She asked her husband where he thought they were from. He replied that they were undoubtedly Brazilian; the Portuguese behaved differently, they were less spontaneous. The repressed desires of the last few years emerged in her with such vehemence they almost knocked her down. The mere fact of hearing that language seemed to intoxicate her. She took out her pocket mirror, placed it in front of her face, and put it away again in deep disgust. She looked at the sweaty faces of those young men, their eyes as if lulled to sleep by the heat under long eyelashes, their velvety and dangerous musculature. She enjoyed the harmony created between their speech and the movement of their bodies. The most daring visions began to shake her to a point approaching pain. She bounced up and down in her chair. She turned her gaze to her husband and discovered a pusillanimous old man, indifferent to her desires and her needs, who was trying with a puerile chuckle to pass himself off as a boy, and she told herself that she'd been the biggest fool in the world not to have had one or more lovers during the years she remained cloistered in Cuernavaca waiting for that pitiful nincompoop to show signs of life. She told herself furiously again that if there had ever been a monumental fool in this world, her name was Jacqueline Cascorró, for having waited so long for a good-for-nothing who one day had the gall to believe he was a Rothschild.

She looked again at the young Brazilians. They were peeling their prawns with their fingers. When she saw their greasy hands, their shiny lips, their eager gestures, she felt something akin to an electric shock come over her, a vision as perfect as the one she'd glimpsed many years before when she broke a crab leg and heard the popping of a champagne cork. She knew that the only way to kill Nicolás Lobato would be with poison. The doctors would certify that the cause of death was shellfish poisoning. Her leg brushed against her husband's; with a furtive movement she put her hand on his thigh; she wanted to slide it toward his groin but didn't dare. The look that she transfixed on Nicolás Lobato's face as she caressed his leg was charged with an accumulation of demented hatred.

CHAPTER 7

MONTHS LATER, A MAN AND woman entered a restaurant in Villa del Mar. The man was pushing a wheelchair in which the woman was sitting. They arrived at a table and the man, with great care, helped the woman stand and move to a regular chair. It was, of course, Jacqueline and Nicolás Lobato. It was impossible to hear their conversation. His gesticulations as well as his expressions were reminiscent of those that a father might employ to admonish and, at the same time, calm a willful little girl. Jacqueline barely reacted. She could barely open one eye; its drooping eyelid was purplish and blood-red, which would lead anyone to think that the woman shouldn't have left the house that day. Her lips were monstrously swollen. She barely responded to her husband's words, raising instead her shoulders contemptuously or refuting something with clumsy movements of her head. They were celebrating another wedding anniversary.

Coyoacán, March–November 1990

Sergio Pitol Demeneghi (1933–2018) was one of Mexico's most influential and well-respected writers, born in the city of Puebla. He studied law and philosophy in Mexico City and spent many years as a cultural attaché in Mexican embassies and consulates across the globe, including Poland, Hungary, Italy, and China. He is renowned for his intellectual career in both the field of literary creation and translation, with numerous novels, stories, criticisms, and translations to his name. Pitol is an influential contemporary of the most well-known authors of the Latin American "Boom," and began publishing his works in the 1960s. In recognition of the importance of his entire canon of work, Pitol was awarded the two most important prizes in the Spanish language world: the Juan Rulfo Prize in 1999 (now known as the FIL Literary Award in Romance Languages) and the Cervantes Prize, the most prestigious Spanish-language literary prize, often called the "Spanish language Nobel," in 2005.

G. B. Henson is the author of eleven book-length translations, including works by Cervantes laureates Sergio Pitol (published by Deep Vellum) and Elena Poniatowska. His translations have appeared variously in *Words Without Borders*, *Asymptote*, *Latin American Literature Today*, *World Literature Today*, *Granta*, and the *New England Review*. He holds a PhD from the University of Texas at Dallas and is a visiting professor of Spanish translation at the Middlebury Institute of International Studies in Monterey. George was a 2021–2023 Tulsa Artist Fellow in literary translation.

Mark Haber was born in Washington, D.C. and grew up in Florida. His debut novel, *Reinhardt's Garden* (2019), was longlisted for the PEN/Hemingway Award. His second novel, *Saint Sebastian's Abyss* (2022), was named a best book of 2022 by the New York Public Library and *Literary Hub*. His most recent novel, *Lesser Ruins* (2024), was longlisted for the Republic of Consciousness Prize. Most recently, Mark was appointed Visiting Professor at Freie Universität Berlin during the 2024/2025 winter semester. Mark lives in Minneapolis.

www.ingramcontent.com/pod-product-compliance
Lightning Source LLC
Jackson TN
JSHW022335131025
92428JS00001B/1